THE HORSES OF
HALF MOON RANCH

MIDNIGHT LADY

Jenny Oldfield

Published by Sourcebooks Jabberwocky, an imprint of Sourcebooks, Inc.
P.O. Box 4410, Naperville, Illinois 60567-4410
(630) 961-3900
Fax: (630) 961-2168
www.sourcebooks.com

Originally published in Great Britain in 1999 by Hodder Children's Books.

Library of Congress Cataloging-in-Publication Data

Oldfield, Jenny.
   Midnight Lady / Jenny Oldfield.
      p. cm.—(Horses of Half Moon Ranch ; bk. 5)
   Summary: Thirteen-year-old Kirstie gets into trouble when she tries to help a mistreated horse escape from a neighboring ranch.
   [1. Horses—Fiction. 2. Ranch life—Colorado—Fiction. 3. Animals—Treatment—Fiction. 4. Colorado—Fiction.] I. Title.
   PZ7.O4537Mi 2009
   [Fic]—dc22
                              2008039732

Printed and bound in the United States of America.
VP 10 9 8 7 6 5 4 3 2

1

"…Copper Bottom and Steel Dust; that's where it all began," Hadley Crane said as he backed the trailer out of the parking lot at San Luis Sale Barn.

"Yeah, like, I know exactly what you're talking about!" Lisa Goodman raised her eyebrows at Kirstie Scott. The reversing trailer raised a cloud of dust, which blew grit into the girls' eyes. It was late afternoon and the baking sun was sinking low in a clear blue sky.

"Two sires," Hadley went on. The head wrangler at Half Moon Ranch positioned the trailer to wait in line at the wide exit onto Route 27. "Copper Bottom and Steel Dust started a specialist breed of horse way back in the 1930s."

"What was special about them?" Kirstie could hear the three young horses they'd just bought stamping impatiently inside the metal trailer. She fanned her face with the sale program, then pulled down the peak of her baseball cap to shade her eyes.

"Easy to keep. Good feet. Small. Fast." Tersely, Hadley listed the strong points of the breed of horse used by the ranchers in the West. "Mighty fast, as a matter of fact. You put a postage-stamp-sized saddle on one of those guys, set him on a sprint track around the outside of a rodeo arena, and he'd blast out of that starting gate like a bullet out of a gun."

Kirstie grinned at Lisa. Get Hadley talking about his favorite subject, and there was no stopping him. The normally silent old ranch hand could ramble on for ages. "Isn't that why they're called quarter horses?" she asked, as their tall vehicle eased out onto the road.

"Sure." He signaled left and followed the sign that read: Minesville 8 miles, Renegade 3 miles. "Those races were no more than a quarter of a mile long. The horse never drew breath the whole time he was sprinting. He slowed up over the finish line and realized he might be kinda short of breath out there. But there was nothing to beat him for a short burst of speed. Short horse, or quarter horse. And it's all because of Copper Bottom and Steel Dust."

"Hmm." Lisa was impressed. She settled back in the passenger seat for the drive down the narrow, straight road to Renegade. "So the three horses we bought for Donna Rose back there, Skeeter, Moonpie, and Midnight Lady, they're all quarter horses?"

Skeeter, the three-year-old black-and-white paint. Strangely named Moonpie, the flea-bitten gray with a rash of brownish markings. Long-limbed, dapple gray Midnight Lady. Kirstie held a picture of them in her mind, their nervousness in the sale barn arena, heads up, ears flicking this way and that in reaction to the unaccustomed noise and bustle.

3

She recalled the paint's high-pitched whinny as Hadley led him up the ramp into the trailer, Moonpie following reluctantly where his more spirited leader had already gone. And the trouble they'd had loading Midnight Lady, who'd objected to the dark steel box and the echo of her hooves as they struck the metal ramp. She'd pulled and strained at the halter rope, until Hadley had switched tactics and offered her a handful of sweet alfalfa hay to tempt the hungry horse inside.

"I guess the paint and the flea-bitten gray are your typical quarter horse," Hadley agreed. "I knew Donna would want to use those two the minute I set eyes on them. Stout hindquarters, deep chests; good ranch horses the both of them."

"What about Midnight Lady?" To Kirstie's eye the dappled gray horse seemed different. Not so stocky—taller, more slender. A lady, in fact.

Hadley took a right, heading off the main road out across a flat plain, away from the Meltwater range of mountains, where he helped Kirstie's mother, Sandy Scott, cope with the hundreds of guest riders who visited Half Moon Ranch each year. At the end of the straight, narrow track lay

Donna Rose's working cattle ranch, the Circle R. "The gray is a grade horse, which means she's been upgraded. She's a mustang crossed with a quarter horse. She's got breeding, but no papers to prove it, if you catch my drift."

"She's wonderful!" Kirstie breathed. *Long legs, long arched neck, a haughty tilt to her head.*

"You would say that!" Lisa joked about her friend's well-known love of every single horse on the planet. "But let's hope Donna thinks so, too." She reminded them of the problem they'd had getting the third horse into the trailer.

Way down the track, the isolated ranch house came into view. It was surrounded by a green sea of prairie grass whispering and shimmering in the wind, making the house itself look like a becalmed wooden boat. Close up, they saw the red tiled roof, the log walls, the overhanging porch —and Donna Rose standing in the doorway ready to greet them.

"Howdy, y'all!" Donna's smile was broad and sparkling white. Her hair was streaked blonde, her turquoise earrings dangled down almost to the wide shoulders of her crisp denim jacket. She wore a white shirt and a big silver buckle on her broad tan leather belt.

"Howdy, ma'am." Hadley stepped from the cab, hitching his leather gloves into the waistband of his worn jeans. He strode to the back of the trailer, ready to unbolt the door and let down the ramp.

"Hey!" Kirstie said to the ranch owner with a shy, awkward smile, while Lisa scrambled past her to follow Hadley.

"You bought me some neat horses?" the glamorous, middle-aged owner of Circle R inquired, stepping down from the porch in her fancy, tooled brown and cream heeled boots.

"We sure hope so!" Lisa's smile matched Donna's in the dazzling department. "Hadley paid a mean price leastways."

"That's why I asked him to do me the favor," Donna went on, smooth as silk, sweet as sugar. She stood to one side, hands on hips, ignoring the dust and the tumbleweed that rolled across the yard in front of the ranch house. Behind her, swinging from the porch was a giant bundle of chili peppers, hung out in the sun to dry. A gnarled pair of stag's antlers were propped to one side of the doorway; probably a hunting trophy from many seasons ago. "Me and Hadley, we go way back. I know he drives a hard bargain!"

The old ranch hand ducked his head. Beneath his wide-brimmed dark Stetson hat and his all-year-round weather-beaten tan, Kirstie could have sworn he was blushing. To hide his embarrassment, he kept busy unloading the horses while Donna talked.

And boy, did she talk.

"When I say way back, I mean we were in high school together," she explained to a still grinning Lisa.

Kirstie frowned and did a double take. Donna Rose was smooth-skinned and young looking, where Hadley was lined and worn. Surely she was years younger! But then, maybe it was the carefully styled hair and glossy pink lipstick that did it.

"Hadley's much older than me, naturally!" Donna continued, as if reading Kirstie's thoughts. Her voice held a teasing lightness. "And if he was the gentleman I believed he was, he'd have been the one to jump right in there and tell you that!"

Schkk...schkk! The heavy bolts slid back and Hadley let down the ramp. Inside the trailer, the three horses stamped and barged.

"He was in tenth grade at San Luis High when I got there. I was Donna Ward back then. All we innocent young gals adored him, he was so tall and handsome!"

"Wow!" Lisa giggled at Kirstie. Hadley handsome?

Ignoring them all, Hadley stomped up the metal ramp into the trailer, unhitched the first horse, and led him out. "Easy, boy, easy!"

Kirstie watched Skeeter clatter down the ramp. The black-and-white horse emerged into the low sunlight head high and staring. His nostrils flared wide, his jaw was tense; sure signs that the journey had disagreed with him.

But Hadley held him firmly on the end of a short rope. He spoke soft words of encouragement. "C'mon, Skeeter, there's a good guy. Ain't nothing here to worry you none."

"What do you think?" Kirstie asked eagerly, the moment Donna Rose stopped talking and switched her attention from the wrangler to the beautiful horse. In the background, she noticed a young man come out of the barn across the yard and head slowly in their direction.

"Pretty!" The lady ranch owner murmured her appreciation. "I like paints. They're my favorite."

"Are you gonna use him as a cutting or a roping horse?" Kirstie wanted to know.

"What's the difference?" Lisa snuck into the pause while Donna contemplated her answer.

"You use a cutting horse in the spring and fall for cutting out from the herd those cows you want to brand and doctor," Kirstie explained quietly. "He's trained to work off a loose rein and respond to your voice. That kind of horse needs a lot of natural savvy."

"And I guess a roping horse is the one you use to chase and lasso the cows with," Lisa put in. "Gee, I'm learning so much!" Up went the dark, ironic eyebrows and the corners of her full mouth.

"You did ask!" Kirstie retaliated. By now the stranger from the barn had joined their small group. He was tall and lean, with a narrow, clean-shaven face and a noticeably big, bony nose. His shirt was bright red, with silver buttons and plenty of fancy over-stitching, and he wore expensive, brand new leather chaps over his tight jeans. Instead of saying hi and joining in the conversation, however, he stood slightly apart, managing to avoid eye contact by concentrating entirely on the three new horses.

"Cutting or roping?" Donna turned to the young newcomer for advice.

The young man studied Skeeter, then shrugged. "Roping, I guess. He's got plenty of muscle in his hindquarters to brace himself and take the weight of a twelve-hundred-pound cow on the end of a rope."

"And how about Moonpie?" Lisa urged as Hadley returned to the trailer and led the more timid gelding down the ramp. He was good as gold, looking out for Skeeter and going meekly where Hadley led him.

"Cutting," came the short reply.

"That means TJ can ride the paint and we give Moonpie to Jesse," Donna decided with a nod of satisfaction. "Which leaves the third bronc for you to train up and ride yourself, Leon!"

They waited eagerly as Hadley tethered Moonpie

next to Skeeter inside a rough stockade formed from thick, upright pine poles, then returned to the trailer for the last horse. Eagerly, that is, except for Leon, the moody young man, who scowled behind Donna's back.

"She's my favorite of the three!" Kirstie told Donna. "Hadley picked her out because she's a grade horse, which means she's part mustang, part quarter horse..." Trotting out Hadley's earlier description, she caught a glimpse of Lisa's rolling eyes and exaggerated, bored yawn. Kirstie got her revenge back by giving her friend a quick, sly dig in the ribs.

"Sounds like she has quite a temper." Donna's dazzling smile faded slightly as the trailer thundered, rattled, and rocked. Hadley was having a tough time getting Midnight Lady down the ramp.

"I told you to let me drive into San Luis and buy my own horse," the man called Leon grumbled.

"You may be manager here, Leon, but I'd trust Hadley to make the right choice every time." Donna put him in his place, then smiled once more in her old friend's direction. Now all eyes were on the back of the trailer and tension was mounting. "Ever since my husband, Don, passed on three winters back, Hadley's been an absolute angel to me!"

Hadley, an angel? Kirstie noticed that this time Lisa's eyes rolled almost out of sight. She noticed, too, that Leon's scowl had deepened after Donna's latest tactless remark. But there was no time to dwell on it, as the drama of getting the reluctant bronc out of the trailer developed.

"Kirstie, see if you can grab a bunch of hay and stand where she can see it!" Hadley yelled from inside.

Thinking fast, she pointed to the barn, and when Donna nodded back at her, she sped off to get the hay. Grabbing a bunch from a net hanging in the doorway, she returned as fast as she could and positioned herself with outstretched arms at the base of the ramp.

Inside the trailer, Midnight Lady was still kicking up a mighty fuss. She was snorting and stamping, eyeing the ramp as if it was a treacherous trap ready to collapse the moment she set foot on it. Hadley was the main enemy, trying to snare her; Kirstie was laying temptation in her way; and the sky itself looked like it might fall on her if she so much as ventured outside.

"Easy!" Hadley cooed and cajoled with his deep, growling voice. "Easy, girl. Ain't no one gonna harm you!" He'd deliberately eased off the tension on the lead rope and waited patiently for the mare to calm down. "You take your time, come out when you want to. Kirstie down there's got a mighty tasty bunch of alfalfa for you to chew on soon as you're good and ready."

Kirstie smiled and nodded. "Sure. This here's a great ranch: your new home. Ain't nothing bad gonna happen out here."

Midnight Lady stopped snorting and kicking and started to listen. Her pricked ears picked up the sound of the wind rustling through long grass, the miles of silence.

"Easy," Kirstie murmured. She saw the young mare give one last shake of her head and a final swish of her silky white tail. Her nostrils caught the scent of the sweet alfalfa. Dipping her head and stretching out her neck, she inched forward.

Kirstie held her hand steady. One step at a time, Midnight Lady eased out of the trailer, her hooves clomping slowly down the ramp, Hadley at her side. Low shafts of golden sunlight hit her dappled coat as she emerged, emphasizing her sleek flanks and rounded rump, her fine, athletic form.

Then, at last, she was nibbling hay from Kirstie's hand, her soft mouth nipping at the golden strands, her teeth chomping and grinding quietly. Kirstie backed slowly away, enticing the horse clear of the trailer. She gave a sideways glance at Donna, Lisa, and Leon and a short smile. *See! Everything's gonna be fine. All you need is a little patience.*

"Pretty!" Donna stepped forward to inspect her latest buy. "That's a classy little mare you picked out, Hadley!"

But before she had a chance to examine Midnight Lady in detail, Leon, her scowling manager, cut in. "Jesse, TJ, get out here quick!" he yelled toward the barn. "Bring tarps and extra ropes!"

The harsh sound of his voice made the gray mare raise her head and tug at the halter rope.

Two men came running. One was medium height and build with slicked back fair hair. The other was chubby-faced and unshaven. His black hair was cut short. Both were around twenty years

14

old, carrying coils of rope and small squares of heavy canvas cloth.

Alarmed at the sudden change of mood, Kirstie shot a question at Hadley, who was having to hang on for all he was worth to a spooked Midnight Lady. "What are the tarpaulins for?"

"Later!" Hadley said through gritted teeth. "I got my hands full right now!"

Midnight Lady skittered sideways, away from the new men, pulling Hadley after her. Her eyes rolled as she barged against the nearby fence, then she shot forward.

"Watch out, this one's a snorter!" Leon yelled. "A real jug-head!"

"Now hold on just a second!" Hadley protested, as Midnight Lady reared up on him. Her hooves flashed down dangerously close to his head. Still he held on tight to the lead rope.

Leon ignored him. "TJ, throw another rope around her neck!" he ordered the round-faced ranch hand.

Roughly TJ obeyed, waiting for the horse to barge herself into a corner before he succeeded in slipping a noose over her head and jerking the rope hard to tighten it.

Midnight Lady squealed and tried to rear.

"There's no need for that!" Kirstie appealed to Donna Rose. "We'd already gotten her to cooperate!"

But it was too late now. The mare was kicking out in panic while TJ pulled on the rope with all his weight.

"Get her into the stockade with the other two!" Leon cried. He strode to the gate, ordering Jesse to flap the square of tarpaulin against the horse's hindquarters. The second ranch hand brought the tarp down on Midnight Lady's back, making her plunge forward in fright. Hadley lost his grip on the lead rope and watched grim faced as the two young hands took over the job of getting the horse into the stockade. Slowly, with much kicking and squealing, they succeeded in steering her through the gate.

"Good job!" Leon cried as he slammed the gate behind the horse.

Sweating and out of breath, TJ and Jesse congratulated each other with a slap of palms.

Kirstie frowned. She heard Lisa give a small, relieved sigh. Donna Rose, meanwhile, was left with no trace of the earlier smile on her carefully made-up face.

"We seem to have got ourselves a problem breaking that bronc," she commented quietly as Hadley strode across the yard toward her.

"Slow and easy," he advised. "You get her to a point where she wants to work for you, and after that you've got no problem."

Nodding hard, Kirstie ran to check that Midnight Lady wasn't harming herself against the rough poles of the stockade fence. She stood on the bottom bar of the gate and peered in to see the gray horse trotting nervously around the small compound, ears laid flat, nostrils flared. She was looking for a way out, switching direction, wheeling and arching her back in fear.

"C'mon, Kirstie!" Lisa called. "Time to go!"

Kirstie glanced over her shoulder to see Hadley climb into the cab of the trailer. She heard him start up the engine, obviously in a hurry to leave. "Gee, I'm sorry!" she whispered as Midnight Lady veered toward her, then slid to a halt and plunged off in another direction. "We never meant for that to happen."

The horse reared and dipped, kicked out at the solid fence, ran on.

"Kirstie!" Lisa yelled a second time.

"It'll be OK, you'll see," she promised the frightened mare. "Give yourself a day or two to settle in. We'll try and get back to see you during the weekend!"

"We're leaving without you!" Lisa warned, following Hadley into the cab.

One last glance. Midnight Lady stopped short, flung back her head and whinnied. Her white mane whipped across her neck as she swung around...trotting again, sliding to a halt in the dust, swerving...running in vain from the loud voices and tight, harsh ropes of her impatient new owners.

2

Early July was high season at Half Moon Ranch, and Kirstie's worries about Midnight Lady were soon pushed to one side by the busy routine of leading dude riders out on the trails, helping to make sure that none of the visitors fell off or got lost on the pine-covered slopes of the Meltwater Range.

"You won't believe what happened today!" she told Lisa over the phone. It was three days after the visit to Circle R and the two friends hadn't had a chance to meet up since. "Today's Sunday, right?

Our first day on Five Mile Creek trail with a bunch of beginners. There's this guy on Crazy Horse, and you know how sweet and easy that horse is. Well, the guy's never been in a saddle in his life. First time, right? Charlie's leading the group, and he tells them to walk nice and slow along the side of the creek. But this tough guy at the end of the line wants to act like a cowboy in front of two other guys from his office back in New Jersey.

"So he ignores Charlie and works Crazy Horse straight into a lope. Crazy Horse takes off like a rocket. The guy bounces all over the place and has to hang on to the saddle horn just to stay put. Crazy Horse thinks, 'I'll show this jug-head,' gallops wide of the bunch, and right into the creek. The water sprays up and smacks the guy right in the face. He yells out, tips backward out of the saddle, and rolls into the creek!"

"Hey!" Lisa laughed and appreciated the scene. "What did Crazy Horse do then?"

"He stopped and stood as if butter wouldn't melt, head to one side like he was asking, 'Hey, what happened? Was it something I did?' The guy stood up waist-deep, with water pouring off the brim of his hat, down his face, everywhere. It was squelching out of his boots every step he took as he climbed up the bank! His office pals were doubled over laughing. Charlie said nothing, but the guy had to go back to the ranch to get a change of clothes while the rest of us rode on."

"And Crazy Horse got the morning off." Lisa giggled. "Smart horse. Speaking of time off, Kirstie, why don't you drive into town this afternoon and drop in at the diner? It's been ages since you came over to my place."

"Sounds good. I heard Matt say he was planning to drive in, so I could get a ride." Kirstie's older brother, Matt, was heading back to Denver to see his girlfriend later that day and could easily drop Kirstie off in San Luis, where Lisa's mom, Bonnie, ran the End of Trail Diner. "Maybe we could even get him to drive us out as far as Renegade, to take a look at the three broncs we bought for the Circle R."

"What's that, a guilty conscience?" Lisa joked.

"No, I kinda had it in mind it'd be nice to see how they're doing…" Kirstie tailed off. "Yeah, guilty conscience," she admitted. "I got this sneaking feeling we let Midnight Lady down the day we dropped her off at Donna's place. I want her to know we care what happens to her."

"Me, too," Lisa agreed. She told Kirstie to fix things up with Matt for a lift out to the ranch, while she made arrangements at her end for her mom to pick them up and drive them back. "See you at two thirty!" she ended, bright and breezy. "And, Kirstie, try not to get too stressed out. Midnight Lady's gonna be just fine, you'll see!"

"Why not bring Lisa back to Half Moon with you?" Sandy Scott called from the ranch house porch. "Tell her she can stay over for a few days if she'd like."

"Thanks, Mom!" Kirstie gave her a smile and a wave as she sank into the passenger seat of Matt's beaten-up, pale blue Chevy. The invitation meant that she and Lisa would be able to ride out together, away from the trails worn smooth by the guests. They would take her own palomino horse, Lucky, use Matt's horse, Cadillac, for Lisa, and head for remote spots like Eden Lake or Bear Hunt Overlook, maybe bushwhacking cross-country through shadowy glades, above the snow line to Eagle's Peak.

She was picturing the scene—the rushing streams, the narrow passes—as Matt drove slowly out of the yard and along the winding dirt road toward Route 5. The car rattled along, washboarding over dry ridges caused by water running across the road during a spring flood. She sat back in her seat as they rounded a bend to the left, tight against a sheer face of brownish red rock.

"What the...!" Matt slammed on the brake.

A cream pickup truck was hurtling toward them, way over their side of the road. A cloud of dust billowed out behind.

"He's not gonna stop!" Kirstie cried. She braced her arms against the dashboard, felt their own car shimmy sideways in a screech of brakes.

The pickup driver saw them, but it was too late. His own brakes went on so hard he lost control, sliding and skidding across their path until the two vehicles came to a crunching, grinding halt. The pickup had hit them head on, to the sound of shattering glass and scraping metal.

"You OK?" Matt turned to Kirstie before he opened his door.

She nodded. "Fine. No problem." Which was more than could be said about Matt's car. Steam was rising from its hood, the windshield shattered into a thousand tiny fragments.

"If that's Chuck Perry, I'll kill him!" Matt seemed to have recognised the pickup. "The guy drives like a maniac. I'm always telling him to take it easy along this road!" Getting out of his smashed car, he strode to confront the other driver.

Chuck Perry was the shoer from Minesville who came to Half Moon Ranch once a month to shoe the horses. It was true he was a reckless driver, as the beat-up condition of his often-changed pickups proved. And yes, Kirstie saw that Matt's guess was correct as the driver emerged from his vehicle and she recognized the short, squat, mustached figure of the farrier.

"Where's the fire?" Matt demanded, standing hands on hips.

"No fire. Just a dozen horses to shoe and three different places to be in at any one time," Chuck snapped back, turning in dismay to look at his busted radiator and smashed fender. "I gotta finish here and get over to Circle R before sundown. Now look what happened!"

"It kinda puts out a few plans of my own," Matt pointed out, his temper cooling once he got over the shock. If he'd been expecting Chuck to apologize, he would have been sorely disappointed. Instead, the tough, muscular shoer was winding himself up into a frustrated rage.

"How am I gonna do my work?" he demanded, pointing to the portable forge and box of tools in the back of his pickup. "And if I don't shoe those horses, I don't get paid. I got bills up to here." A hand gesture above his head showed Kirstie and Matt that he was snowed under by debt.

"OK, OK." Matt began to think on the shoer's behalf, seemingly willing to forget whose fault the accident had been. Kirstie thought this was very big of him, considering how grumpy she felt about not getting to Lisa's on time. And it wasn't even her car that had been totaled. "What do you say we walk back to the ranch and get Hadley to tow you in?" he went on to suggest. "That way, you get your equipment in place and you can put shoes on our horses."

Grumbling and sighing through his mustache, Chuck Perry agreed. Within half an hour, with Hadley's help, the bend in the road was cleared and the farrier hard at work outside the barn.

Kirstie, too, had rearranged her plans. "Hadley says he'll drive Chuck to Circle R late this afternoon," she told Lisa on the phone. "It just so happens that he's down to put new shoes on Moonpie, Skeeter, and Midnight Lady after he's finished here. That works well for us, as a matter of fact."

"Sure." Lisa didn't care how they got to Circle R. She was her usual, laid-back self.

"Not so good for Matt though." Kirstie could see her brother sitting dejectedly astride the fence overlooking the empty corral. It was already well past three and he'd had to call up Lachelle in Denver to tell her he wasn't going to make it after all. "He's a star-crossed lover," she told Lisa.

"Like poor old Romeo!" Lisa laughed unsympathetically. They'd both read the play and seen the film. "'Parting is such sweet sorrow!'"

"Yeah. Except Matt and Lachelle; they never even got together!" And Matt was no Romeo, and Lachelle no Juliet for that matter. Too into the workings of boring car engines and the latest shade of lipstick for that, though Kirstie would never dare say so.

"So we get to see Midnight Lady again, after all!" Lisa said happily. She'd dumped a bag containing nightclothes and riding gear into the back of Hadley's pickup and climbed in beside Kirstie.

It was five o'clock on a long, lazy Sunday afternoon. Lisa's mom, Bonnie, had taken a quick break from serving coffee and food and come out onto the sidewalk to see her daughter off, snatching a few words with Hadley as he leaned out of the driver's window.

"You be sure and say hi to Donna for me," she made him promise. "She was in here the other day, singing your praises over three horses you bought for her. Couldn't say enough. If I didn't know better, I'd say Mrs. Rose was a tiny little bit sweet on you, Hadley Crane!"

In the back of the truck, squashed in beside Chuck Perry's forge and toolbox, Lisa and Kirstie broke up.

"She wouldn't hear a word against you!" Bonnie

Goodman insisted, playing the situation for all it was worth. She was enjoying the wrangler's blushes. "Leon Franks stood alongside her, mumbling something about one of the horses being vicious, but Donna knocked him straight back…"

"When was this exactly?" Kirstie cut in, suddenly serious when she caught the word "vicious."

"Let me see…this was Friday." Bonnie ran a hand through her dark curls as Hadley signaled to pull out onto Main Street. But first he let a car park up in front of him, outside True West, the San Luis gift shop selling handtooled leather cigar boxes, custom-made Stetsons, and antique wagon wheel chandeliers. "Why, what's the problem?" Lisa's mom caught the change of mood.

"Nothing." Lisa smoothed things over. "See you in a couple of days!"

They were off up the street, past the gas station and convenience store. Chuck Perry sat stiffly beside Hadley, his face refusing to crack a smile. The old ranch hand himself was still recovering from Bonnie's far-fetched theory about him and Donna Rose.

"When did Donna lose her husband?" Lisa asked

Kirstie, enjoying the wind in her hair as the truck gathered speed.

"She didn't *lose* him," Kirstie protested. "You make him sound like an old sock in a laundromat. He died. She's been a widow for three-and-a-half years. And no, Hadley never had a wife. Believe me, he just ain't the marrying kind!"

The smile that Donna Rose used on Chuck Perry when the shoer finally showed up to work on her three new horses was a pale shadow in comparison with the dazzler she turned on Hadley as he got out of the red Dodge and sat himself down on the porch swing at Circle R.

"I'd like you to check out my five other working horses while you're here," she told the farrier. "TJ and Jesse just brought them in from the meadow for you to take a look at. They're in the barn right now."

Chuck grunted and nodded.

"What got into him? He's like a bear with a sore head." Donna's earrings shook and caught the light as she laughed at Chuck's retreating form.

"Major surgery needed to his main method of

transportation," Kirstie reported. "Serious damage to his collateral."

"His truck's been in a crash," Lisa translated. "He totaled it completely."

"How are Skeeter and Moonpie?" Swiftly Kirstie changed the subject to what really interested her as she spotted Leon Franks on horseback. The ranch manager pretended that he hadn't seen the visitors as he drove a black-and-white cow and calf into the tall stockade.

"They're doing great," Donna assured her. "Leon's been working with them. He put saddles on their backs for the first time earlier today. Both of them took it without so much as a single buck. I tell you, when it comes to breaking broncs, Leon's your man!"

Kirstie listened and nodded. "That's good," she said cautiously, then turned to Hadley. The word "breaking" somehow bothered her. "Ain't that good news?"

"Sure, if they're gentle broke," he replied. "If those horses are working out of willingness and not fear, I'd say that Leon did a great job saddling them up so quick."

"How would you tell the difference?" It was Lisa's turn to ask a question.

"Yes, you're the expert!" Donna said brightly. "C'mon, Hadley, give us the benefit of your years of experience!"

He looked up from under the brim of his hat. "A gentle broke horse acts like he's your friend. He responds to kindness. If you break him with force, there's fear in all his movements. He spends his life thinking you're gonna hurt him with ropes and whips, and he's most likely right; you're the kind of rider who'll give him more pain the second he steps out of line. So you see it in his eyes mainly; his slave look, his burn of resentment."

"Or *hers*," Kirstie said quietly. But the mood had changed so much that she didn't dare to go ahead and ask after Midnight Lady.

And anyway, Donna Rose had cheerfully missed the point. "When I saw your truck coming up the track, I asked Jesse and TJ to saddle Moonpie and Skeeter to give you a small demonstration of where we're at," she told them proudly. "They should be about ready by this time. Would you like to come through the barn to the corral around the back?"

Nodding and trying to squash their uneasiness, Lisa and Kirstie followed the ladylike owner.

"C'mon, you, too!" Donna waited at the barn door for an even more reluctant Hadley.

He came slowly across the yard, stopping to say a few words to Chuck Perry in the area by the barn where the sparks flew from the anvil and the shoer hammered metal into the correct shape and size for one of Donna's roping horses who was tethered nearby. By the time Hadley joined Lisa, Kirstie and Donna in the corral, Jesse and TJ were ready to mount their broncs.

Skeeter came in first, ahead of Moonpie. TJ walked him confidently out of another door to the barn and into the empty corral. Skeeter's head was up, his eyes staring. Kirstie noticed a raised mark across the white flash that ran the length of his bony face and a patch of bright yellow antiseptic paint on one of his white front socks. But he stood quietly enough while TJ checked his cinch strap and prepared to mount.

Likewise Moonpie, when he was led into the corral by Jesse. The flea-bitten gray seemed to be tense; his tail was tight against his rump, his back slightly arched under the unaccustomed weight of the saddle. But he didn't protest as his rider grabbed a fistful of white mane and roughly hauled himself skyward.

"Hmm," was all Hadley said as both junior ranch hands landed heavily on the horses' backs.

Not much, but enough for Kirstie. Hadley's "Hmm" said it all. For a moment she closed her eyes and drew a sharp breath.

"See how docile they both are!" said a pleased Donna Rose.

Jesse and TJ gave Moonpie and Skeeter a firm dig with their spurs, jolting the young horses into forward motion. The geldings felt the cold bite of metal across their tongues as the reins suddenly tightened. Back went their heads, eyes rolling. But they obeyed the command to walk on.

"*Too* docile!" Lisa murmured under her breath.

Tears came to Kirstie's eyes as she witnessed the scene and tried to imagine what it must have taken to break these two horses' spirits. Ropes and tarps, whips and spurs. Hobbled legs, blows to head and belly. She'd read about the cruel methods men sometimes used to subdue an unbroken horse.

"Leon's done a fine job, don't you think?" the unwary ranch owner gushed, taking the evidence at face value. After all, there were riders on the geldings' backs, and the animals showed no sign of protesting. "We'll have these two at work in time for the fall roundup, no problem!"

With an effort, Kirstie summoned her voice to speak the question that had been on the tip of her tongue since they arrived at Circle R. She glanced back at the barn and out into the empty meadow beyond the corral. With the sound of hammer against anvil ringing in her ears, and with the sight of two cruelly broken horses parading before her, she found the courage to ask, "What about Midnight Lady?"

Sparks flew in her mind, there were hammer blows against her heart, as she prepared herself for Donna Rose's answer.

3

"Midnight Lady is a different story," Donna admitted. "We guess she must have been the lead mare in the bunch where she was reared."

"Meaning what?" Lisa asked.

With her heart thudding, turning her back on the corral and looking around the barn for a sight of the dapple gray horse, Kirstie hardly heard the reply.

"Meaning she's harder to break than Moonpie and Skeeter."

"Because she's more strong-willed?" Lisa pressed.

Donna gave a hollow laugh. "You could say that. Leon would call her more ornery and stubborn."

There was no sign of the horse herself. Kirstie walked the length of a row of empty stalls and came face to face with Leon Franks. Sharp knife in hand, he looked up from his task of breaking open a bale of hay. The expression of annoyance on his angular face, the cold gleam in his gray eyes, made her edge away.

"Kirstie, if you see Leon in there, would you please tell him I'd like to speak with him!" Donna's voice reached them from outside the barn door.

"I hear you!" the ranch manager called back, brushing past Kirstie as he slid the knife into his belt. He strode the length of the barn without looking back.

"Hey, Leon, tell these good people how we're handling the problem with Midnight Lady," Donna went on. "Explain your method of breaking her. What do you call it, sacking out?"

Kirstie felt another jolt and a heightening of her unease. She lingered in the dark barn, unwilling to listen to Leon's reply.

"That's some bronc you bought," he told Hadley with fake jokiness. "Nice looking mare, I give you that. But she turns out to be a real mankiller."

"How come you need the sacks?" Hadley didn't fall for Leon's upbeat tone. His question was brief and suspicious.

Kirstie hung back, still looking for the horse. Through the frame of the wide doorway she could see Jesse and TJ riding a subdued Moonpie and Skeeter around the corral and the huddle of spectators discussing the sacking out process.

"We use tarps, not sacks," Leon explained. "Good, heavy canvas. Once we get close enough to the horse to put on a head collar and tie her down, a couple of us move in and throw the heavy canvas over her back, around her legs, to give her the biggest scare we can. It don't hurt her, just makes her jump. She wonders what hit her, but she's tied fast and she's not running nowhere. Sure, she pulls and kicks. But in the end she understands; there ain't no use fighting it, she might as well give in."

"That's all we've done so far," Donna told Hadley. "It takes a few days' work to get her to that stage."

"To break her spirit?" Lisa put in.

Inside the barn, Kirstie grimaced and went on searching. She turned into a dark stall beyond the hay store and stopped dead.

There was a bed of soiled straw, a bucket of water, a tethered horse struggling to rise from its knees.

Gradually her eyes grew used to the gloom. "Midnight Lady!"

The horse's head swayed from side to side, her legs were too weak to push her up. She sank down.

Kirstie turned and ran. "Come quick!" she yelled to the others. "I found her. There's something wrong with her!" The strong sunlight hit her in the face as she darted out of the barn.

"Kirstie, cool it!" Lisa grabbed her by the arm. "Who did you find? What are you talking about?"

"Midnight Lady! She's real sick!" Gasping for breath, she pulled away. "Call the vet, quick!"

Leon shook his head. "No need for that."

"What do you mean? She can't even stand. If you don't believe me, come and look!"

"I said it's OK," Leon insisted. "I just gave her a quick shot, that's all."

Kirstie shook her head as if to clear her confusion.

She started back into the barn, then turned to face him. "What kind of a shot?"

He shrugged. "A sedative to make her quiet, let the shoer get near her."

"How long will it last?" Kirstie couldn't get the image of a desperate Midnight Lady sinking back into the straw out of her mind.

"Just a few minutes. Enough time for Chuck to fit a set of shoes without being kicked to blazes. She'll come around soon enough." The manager's laid-back manner was intended to show the others that Kirstie was making a fuss over nothing as usual. With another shrug he turned his back and went to see if the shoer was ready for the sedated mare.

So, not only did Leon Franks think it was OK to scare a horse half to death with his primitive breaking-in method, he also considered it fine to drug her into a feeble stupor! Kirstie looked daggers at him as he exchanged words with Chuck Perry then hurried back into the barn to see if Midnight Lady was ready to be fetched.

"Don't shake your head like that," Donna told Hadley. "I know you think Leon's way of working is a little—what shall we say—direct—"

"...Old-fashioned," Hadley interrupted. "Guys were working that way with horses, sacking them out, hobbling them, wearing them down with fear, when I was a kid. I thought it had died out over the last few years, so it beats me where young Leon learned to do it."

"Way out in Wyoming." Donna warned them to move aside as her manager led a lethargic Midnight Lady into the yard.

The horse was still heavily doped and unsteady on her legs, hardly aware of what was happening when the briskly businesslike shoer stood alongside and lifted each of her legs in turn. He matched metal shoes against her hooves, gave his forge an extra blast of heat from the canister of gas connected to it. Flames belched out, making Midnight Lady flinch and stagger.

"That's where Leon worked before I hired him for Circle R earlier this year," Donna explained. "He's known horses all his life, lived on a ranch way out on the state's eastern plains. The sacking out method's been handed down from generation to generation, and Leon reckons it works much better than any of the modern, horse whisperer stuff."

She pointed to the corral where TJ and Jesse were dismounting from Skeeter and Moonpie. "And there's the evidence in front of our very eyes!"

"B-but!" Lisa grimaced as Chuck hammered the red-hot shoes onto the gray mare's feet. There was the smell of singed hoof, the grating sound of a metal rasp.

"Shh!" Kirstie warned. There were giant *buts* in her own mind, too, yet she had just realized the sense of not openly challenging the ranch owner. Donna Rose might look and sound like a fragile flower, easily swayed, but Kirstie detected a hard edge, too.

"Look at it this way," she told them. "It's a battle of wills. Man against horse. And the horse is twelve-hundred pounds of muscle with a brain the size of a can of corn. What are you gonna do? Match him pound for pound? No way. Like Leon says, you use your superior brainpower to fool him into thinking you're the boss. Tactics is what it's all about."

"Hmm," Hadley said again. He tilted his hat back.

"You want him to show you?" Donna was more than willing to prove her point once more.

"Right now?" Kirstie frowned.

"Sure. Leon's planning another session before sundown. Why not watch while Chuck shoes Moonpie and Skeeter?"

Before they could object, Donna went ahead and made arrangements with Leon.

"I'm not sure I want to see this," Lisa whispered to Kirstie as the ranch manager led a groggy, newly shod Midnight Lady into the corral.

"I *know* I don't!" she hissed back. Secretly she prayed that the horse would disprove Leon Franks's cruel theory by fighting back. Yet that would lead to pain. So no, she hoped Midnight Lady would submit. Oh, but that would be sad, to see a beautiful creature's spirit broken! *Confrontation. Battle. Winners and losers.* Her mind whirled; she squeezed her eyes tight shut and wished for it all to go away.

But when she opened them, there was Leon Franks in the corral with ropes and tarps. Midnight Lady was already tethered to a post as he tied a corner of one square of tarpaulin to the end of a rope. The sight sent the mare kicking and rearing, plunging this way and that. The veins in her neck swelled up, her eyes bulged.

Whack! Leon flung the tarp over her hindquarters. It landed with a heavy smack.

Midnight Lady pulled away as if her life depended on escaping from under the tarp. She butted and bit, kicked and bucked.

He dragged it clear, stooped to pick it up, threw it again.

Once more the horse went crazy.

Lisa turned away. Hadley frowned but said nothing. Kirstie looked on in horror.

"Now watch him use the rope to lasso her hind leg!" Donna told them. "He'll tighten the noose, pull the leg clear of the ground and fix the other end of the rope in a second noose around her neck. See, now she's well and truly hobbled!"

Kirstie felt she could hardly breathe, as if the noose was tightening around her own neck, as she saw Midnight Lady struggle bravely, pitifully on three legs to resist the tarp as it landed yet again on her back.

"But it's hurting her!" Lisa protested.

"Only a little." Donna assured them that the horse would soon learn to give in.

"There's a rope burn around her back leg!"

Donna ignored the protest. "Watch. See how the fight's being driven out of her."

It was true; Midnight Lady's kicks were more feeble. The hobble strained the muscles in her leg and neck, made her groan with pain.

Give in! Kirstie pleaded silently. Submission was the only way of making this torture stop. At a certain point the terrorized mare would have to recognize the fact.

Five minutes went by, then ten. Leon persisted in throwing the tarp and tightening the hobble with cold determination.

"Give in!" Lisa whispered out loud.

The horse's head was low, her sides heaved with exhaustion. Now, when the tarp landed on her back, she couldn't summon the energy to buck it off.

"OK, enough!" Donna decided at last. "End of session."

Leon showed no reaction. He simply gathered up the ropes and tarps, loosened the hobble, and walked away. Midnight Lady was left tethered to the post, trembling miserably in the evening sun.

"Unbelievable!" Lisa cried.

After the sacking out demonstration, as soon as Chuck had finished his work, Donna had taken him and Hadley into the ranch house for coffee. Leon, TJ, and Jesse were nowhere to be seen.

"I mean, really...I cannot believe it!" Furious, shocked, unable to find the words to match how she felt about the treatment of the horse, Lisa paced up and down the corral.

Kirstie could hardly bear to look at Midnight Lady.

"That they do this to her and then leave her standing here. It's disgusting!" Lisa kicked a post, turned and strode back. "Why didn't Hadley do something?"

"It's not his horse," Kirstie said quietly. Nothing in the world could be sadder than seeing an animal lose her will to fight. It was as if the flame of life went out.

"Even so!" Lisa's eyes blazed.

"Donna's the boss around here. She believes in it."

"Yeah, and since when were you so reasonable? I thought you'd feel the same way I do!"

"I do, believe me." Slowly, cautiously, Kirstie was moving closer to the exhausted horse. Defeat was written over every inch of Midnight Lady's trembling, sweating body: in her hanging head, her lank white mane, her dull eye. "You know almost the worst thing?" she whispered to Lisa, as she paused and quietly watched. "It's that this feels like my fault!"

"No way." Suddenly Lisa stopped being angry. She stared at Kirstie. "You couldn't know this would happen. No one could."

"It still feels bad. Like, this wouldn't be happening if we hadn't picked her out to come to Circle R. It means we let her down in some way."

"That doesn't make any sense!"

Kirstie glanced at her friend with the ghost of a smile. "Like you say, since when was I reasonable, especially when it comes to horses?" Turning back to Midnight Lady, she noticed that her head was coming up a little, and her ears were beginning to pay attention to the sound of their voices. "Saying sorry might not make any difference," she told the horse softly. "But I am awful sorry."

"Now I *know* you're crazy! Crazy girl talks to horse."

"I'd rather be crazy." Rather talk to horses than people who saw life as a battle of wills. Rather reach out a hand like she was doing now and let the animal get used to her scent, the sound of her voice.

"Take it easy," Lisa whispered when she saw how close Kirstie had got. "Watch out she doesn't bite!"

"You won't bite me, will you?" Kirstie moved in and slid her hand gently down Midnight Lady's neck. The gray coat was clammy, the muscles still quivering. But Kirstie's touch seemed to soothe her and she turned her head.

"Honest to goodness, Kirstie, you gotta go easy." Concerned for her safety, Lisa advised her to back off. "That horse could turn mean any second!"

"No, you won't. Show Lisa you're no mankiller, whatever they say about you." Slowly, slowly, she eased her hand up and down the horse's neck, across her shoulder, along the curve of her back.

Midnight Lady shifted her weight. Her quivering muscles began to relax.

Look softly, smile, show her what it means to be her friend. Kirstie moved in even closer, rubbing her coat with both hands, stroking her cheek, scratching her nose.

"Hey." Lisa's frown melted, her voice was breathy with disbelief. "Can you believe it? You two are bonding!"

Kirstie nodded. Her words, her body language had managed to convince Midnight Lady that she meant no harm.

The beautiful, forgiving mare pushed her head against Kirstie's shoulder and nudged her.

"Yeah!" She leaned her face against the soft, warm neck. "I want you to know: you and me, we're definitely on the same side!"

4

On the right day, in the right frame of mind, Half Moon Ranch was heaven on earth.

The soaring, swooping horizon of Eagle's Peak and other distant mountains of America's Great Divide could whisk away all troubled thoughts. Green meadows were dotted with blue columbines, forested slopes gave shade to calypso orchids, the banks of clear streams glowed with golden marsh marigolds.

Lisa's two summer days at the ranch took the girls out at dawn, when the sky was eggshell blue, before the sun touched Hummingbird Rock. With fingers still slow with sleep and heads dozy from the warmth of their beds, they fumbled with buckles to get saddles on Lucky and Cadillac. The horses nudged at them for a handful of special oat feed from the tub inside the barn door, which Kirstie would bring in two big handfuls. Crested jays perched on the corral fence would watch greedily for spilled crumbs, then, with a flash of vivid blue wings, dart to the ground to pick up seeds.

Then, with the horses' cinches tightened and bridles on, the girls would head out along Five Mile Creek, past the jeep road. They would choose the climb up Bear Hunt Trail, through the tall ponderosa pines to Red Eagle Lodge, where they could turn and look down on Half Moon Ranch in miniature. It was fun to spot the red roofs of the log cabins, the handkerchief-sized square of green lawn, the long barn and tack room, and the bunkhouse where Hadley and Charlie slept.

Or they might take a different route, the favorite Meltwater Trail, which took them through the narrow pass called Fat Man's Squeeze, where granite rocks formed a tall ravine then opened out onto

Dead Man's Canyon and, towering above that, the sheer gray cliff of Miners' Ridge.

Whatever they decided, Lucky and Cadillac bore them steadily. No track was too steep to climb, no creek flowed too fast for them to cross. Kirstie's palomino led the way, while sturdy, stately Cadillac followed. Stopping to rest in the midday sun, coming home in the cool of the evening, Lucky's almost golden coat shone like silk. Beside him, passing quietly through the shadow of an overhanging rock or under the thick branches of dark pine trees, Cadillac's cream color made him seem ghostly and strange.

"It's hard to believe Cadillac was ever like Midnight Lady," Lisa murmured. It was Tuesday evening; her visit was almost over. Tomorrow she must go back to town.

"Huh?" Kirstie closed the gate of Red Fox Meadow and leaned on the fence to watch Lucky and Cadillac lower their heads to graze quietly. Working out the connection, a flicker of a frown appeared on her face. She didn't want her head filled up with pictures of Donna Rose's horse. Right now she would rather concentrate on nice, easy things.

"Or Lucky either," Lisa persisted. "I mean, can you imagine them before they were broken?"

"I hate that word!" It was no good; she was seeing flashes of Midnight Lady bucking and kicking, of ropes and tarps, and of Leon Franks's cold gray stare. "Broken means beaten. I hate it!"

"Hey, it wasn't me; I didn't invent it!" Lisa set off suddenly toward the ranch house. She stuffed her hands into her jeans pockets and hunched her shoulders. "Excuse me for breathing!"

Kirstie sighed and followed. "Sorry."

"Forget it."

"No, really. I am sorry. Listen, Lisa, I get an awful feeling in my stomach whenever I think about Midnight Lady. When we got to know her better, just before we left Circle R on Sunday night, I sensed she'd really begun to trust us—"

"*You!*" Lisa interrupted her. "Not us. It was you she trusted."

"Whatever." Kirstie walked on, head down, deep in thought and struggling with her sense of helplessness. "It's real mean not to take an interest. Like, maybe we should call Donna, ask how Midnight Lady's doing…" It wasn't enough, but it was something.

"Yeah." Lisa slowed her pace. "Say, how am I gonna get into San Luis tomorrow morning?"

"In the red pickup. Matt finally gets to go to Denver, so he can drop you off at your place on the way. Why do you ask?"

One foot on the porch step, glancing back at the golden pink horizon, Lisa made a nervous suggestion. "Maybe we could both go. We could ask Matt to drive us on as far as Donna's place, just call in there unannounced."

"Are you serious?"

"Why not?"

"Without being invited?"

Lisa opened her eyes wide. "Yeah! So they're not expecting us, so they can't give us any corny stuff about Midnight Lady being fine, thank you very much!"

"We could see for ourselves how she's getting on?" Kirstie didn't want to, yet she did. She thought she knew the depressing answer even before they went, couldn't imagine that another visit would make any difference. And yet...

Lisa waited impatiently for an answer.

"OK," she said at last. "You win. I'll ask Matt."

* * *

"I never liked this place," Matt commented as he drove along the run-down main street of Renegade. The white paint on the wooden houses was peeling, old Chevys without wheels stood propped on piles of bricks in driveways. Outside the general store, a skinny black dog begged for food.

The town had a gas station, a couple of bars, and an abattoir, where cows from the local feedlot came for slaughter. Arnie Ash's Abattoir was Renegade's main reason to exist. In spring and fall, ranchers rounded up their cows, selected the ones who were to go for meat, and trucked them along to the feedlot on the wide plain behind the long, straight row of houses. After a week or two of fattening up, the cows made their final short journey into town.

"I sure wouldn't like to live here," Lisa agreed.

No trees, no mountains. Kirstie stared out of the truck window at the weeds growing on the sidewalk, deliberately choosing to look away from the entrance to the slaughterhouse and the bold letters of the sign above the gates. A red traffic light had brought them to a stop. Wind blew sheets of an old newspaper across the street ahead.

"So tell me the plan one more time," Matt said, tapping his fingers impatiently against the steering wheel. At six-foot-two, his long legs and arms seemed cramped inside the cab, and the look in his hazel eyes indicated that he wished he was way down the road to see Lachelle, instead of idling at a traffic light in this hick town.

"You take us to Circle R. We say hi to Donna Rose, then she probably invites us in for coffee. You say yes, we say we'd rather take a look around if that's OK with her." Lisa had the whole thing worked out.

"She's supposed to say fine," Kirstie explained. "So you keep her talking while we snoop in the barn to see if we can spot Midnight Lady."

The lights changed to green. Matt put his foot down on the accelerator, eager to reach the ranch and get it over with. "You mean, I'm part of a plot to spy on a defenseless old lady!"

"Defenseless—*not!*" Lisa snorted.

"Spy—yes!" Kirstie grinned. "It'll only take a few minutes!"

Matt gave his sister a sideways smile and a dubious shake of the head. "Spying... sneaking around someone else's property. Suppose you're not happy with what you see. Then what? Are we into kidnapping horses here, or what?"

Kirstie looked blank. *Trespassing, me? Kidnapping, me? How could you possibly think that?*

Her fake innocence didn't work. As Matt took a left onto Donna Rose's long, straight drive, he demanded a proper answer. "OK, Lisa, give it to me straight. Tell me what I'm getting myself into here!"

"Come into the house and have a cup of coffee," Donna suggested. If she was surprised to see their red Dodge pull up in the yard, she didn't show it.

It was midmorning, midweek. The ranch house door stood open; the bunch of dried chilies hanging in the porch swung in the wind that blew continually off the open plain. It seemed there was nothing but oceans of grass between here and New Mexico.

"Sure, I'll have coffee." Matt winked at Kirstie as he accepted the invitation. Slamming the pickup door, he strode across the yard.

Donna noticed Kirstie and Lisa hang back. "Hey, I guess you girls didn't come all the way out here to drink coffee," she said brightly. Her silver earrings caught the light; the heels of her tan leather boots clicked on the wooden boards.

"Er... no. That is..." Lisa blushed and mumbled.

"We just kinda came along for the ride..." Kirstie did no better.

Donna's smile broadened. "Midnight Lady's in the stockade!"

Wow! Kirstie chewed her lip and frowned. This wasn't in the plan. They were meant to use cunning and stealth to find the horse.

"It doesn't take Einstein to work out she's the reason you came." Warm and friendly, Donna extended the invitation. "Leon's working with her right this minute. Go ahead and take a look."

"No need to worry after all," Matt muttered as he passed the girls.

"Don't be too sure!" Kirstie shot back. What Donna meant by "working" was exactly what she and Lisa had lost sleep over. It would have been better and more according to plan if they'd been able to sneak up on Midnight Lady in a corner of the barn and quietly check her out to see how she was doing.

"Give it to me straight!" Matt had demanded.

"If we find she's been beaten and hurt, we call in the animal welfare people," Lisa had told him. "They charge Leon Franks with cruelty and find Midnight Lady a new home."

"Easy as that?" He'd shaken his head as they'd drawn near the Circle R.

"Why not?" To Kirstie it had looked that simple. There was a law against it. Man mistreats horse. Man gets taken to court. Happy ending for the horse...

So it was a surprise to find Donna so open and welcoming. But there again, the lady was on a different planet as far as the treatment of horses was concerned. Probably when her husband was alive, she'd taken no interest in the workings of the ranch. Now that he was dead, she still left all decisions in her manager's hands.

"I can hear stuff happening in the stockade!" Lisa set off at a run ahead of Kirstie.

There was a shrill whinny, the sound of a whip cracking. The rough fence of pointed pine stakes was too high for the girls to see over, so they had to run around the outside until they came to the gate.

The first thing Kirstie saw was the scarlet of Leon Franks's shirt as he sat in the saddle on one of Circle R's sorrel geldings. The second was the whip in his right hand. Then she saw TJ's heavy figure swinging a tarp on the end of a rope, Jesse standing by with coils of rope. Midnight Lady was tied by a short rope to a post driven into the hard ground. Her front leg was hobbled to a noose around her neck. Kirstie's stomach turned and she felt sick. More sacking out.

"Not again!" Lisa's voice cracked. "It can't still be happening!"

Through the dust raised by the gray mare's struggles, Kirstie could see cruel marks just above her heels where the ropes had worn through the skin in the two days of torture she'd had to endure since they last saw her. "This horse is incredible!" she gasped. So much pain, and still she fought.

With his back to the gate, it was impossible for Franks to have seen the visitors. He yelled orders and moved in with the whip, cracking it close to Midnight Lady's head to make her back off, straight into the thudding weight of the tarp which TJ had launched across her back. She squealed and reared, kicked and staggered onto her knees.

"Move fast, get a saddle on her while she's down!" Franks yelled at Jesse.

The ranch hand obeyed. He wrenched the saddle from a nearby rail, ran with it, and flung its full weight across Midnight Lady's shoulders.

"Fasten the cinch!" Backing off and keeping his distance now, the manager gave Jesse the most dangerous job.

The fair-haired ranch hand hesitated. Though the hobble limited the horse's movements, she could still give a hefty kick with her back legs. He waited for her to collapse forward onto her knees again, then darted in to pull the girth tight. "Don't ask me to get up on her back!" he grunted. "No way am I gonna risk my neck on this snorter!"

"You do what I tell you!" The manager watched coldly as the tightening strap around the horse's belly made her panic. He smiled grimly as she struggled to her feet, bucking and kicking harder than ever, forcing Jesse to leap clear. "I never saw a horse fight so hard!"

"That's it! We call an animal welfare number!" Lisa was white with anger. "Whatever you and Hadley might say about Circle R being able to do what they like with their own horse, we can't let this go on any longer!"

Kirstie gripped the top bar of the gate until her knuckles turned white. It was as if the horrible scene had hypnotized her and fixed her to the spot.

"TJ, you heard what Jesse said. I guess it's up to you." Franks ordered the heavier of the two ranch hands to mount the horse.

The man spat on his hands and rubbed them together. He waited for a lull in the horse's writhing and kicking, then he ran straight at her, and vaulted onto her back. His feet were slotted into the stirrups, his hands gripping her mane before she had time to realize what had happened.

Then, painfully hobbled and tethered as she was, she reacted with fury. She snaked and tossed her head, lurched forward, rocked back onto her haunches, flinging TJ in all directions. Then she launched herself straight up into the air, back arched, until the tether rope jerked hard on her head and pulled her down. TJ yelled with surprise, but held on. Then, instantly, with a straight-legged, forward jump that wrenched and almost toppled the post to which she was tied, Midnight Lady finally unseated her rider.

TJ thudded to the ground. He rolled sideways in the dust as the horse's hooves trampled his hat to a pulp.

Watching every move, Leon's mouth stretched into a thin smile. "Nope. Never seen a horse like it."

Midnight Lady's sides heaved, she staggered on her hobbled leg, her wild face warned she would bite and kick to death anyone who dared to come near.

"Stupid animal!" TJ got shakily to his feet and turned in disgust to his boss. "You tell Donna this horse ain't fit for nothing, you hear!"

"...You tell Donna what?" a voice behind Kirstie and Lisa asked.

They swung around into the glare of the sun to make out the well-groomed figure of the ranch owner herself, slowly followed by Matt.

"Mrs. Rose, you can't let this go on!" Lisa ran to her.

Kirstie turned back to brave Midnight Lady, wishing with every particle of her brain, every ounce of her body, that she could do something—anything—to help!

Donna had ignored Lisa and reached the gate. She was staring at the scene, at the wild-eyed, stamping mare, at the two shaken ranch hands, at Leon Franks sitting coolly on his horse. "Tell Donna what?" she repeated.

"Bad news," Leon drawled, staring over the

stockade fence at the far, flat horizon. "I done my best with this horse, tried every darned thing I know, but it ain't no good."

Brave, brave horse! Kirstie thought. She loved the fierce look in her eye, her spirit's refusal to be broken.

"What are you saying?" Opening the gate, Donna joined her men.

"TJ's right; the mare ain't no good for ranch work," Leon told her. He didn't care one way or the other. It was just a fact.

At first, Donna refused to believe it. "But Hadley chose her. He knows horses inside out!"

"Makes no difference. She's vicious. She got lethal tendencies." Dismounting, the manager took off his black Stetson and wiped his forehead with his sleeve.

"So you give in?" his boss demanded scornfully, one eye on Midnight Lady.

"Yes, Ma'am."

Saying nothing, listening to every word, Lisa nodded hopefully at Kirstie and Matt. At this rate, there wouldn't be any need to call animal welfare; Circle R looked ready to let Midnight Lady go.

"So what do you suggest we do with her?" Donna demanded. "Sell her?"

Leon sniffed and looked at the ground.

"But who'd want a bronc that can't be broken?" The new notion hit Donna hard.

Lisa frowned at Kirstie. "How about Half Moon Ranch buying her?" she whispered.

"Don't even think about it!" Matt warned. He was the hardheaded one in the family, the businessman.

"No one!" Donna answered her own question. "That means we're stuck with a horse we can't use!"

"It happens." Leon shrugged. He looked like he was waiting until Donna had calmed down before he made a suggestion. "Course, no way can we go on feeding a horse who doesn't earn her keep."

Exasperated, looking quickly from one to another in the group until her eyes finally rested on Kirstie, Donna sighed. "It looks like Hadley made an expensive mistake."

Don't blame Hadley, Kirstie thought. *And don't blame Midnight Lady. Leon Franks is the one who's at fault here.*

"There is one way of getting some of your

money back." He cut across Kirstie's dark thoughts to deliver his solution.

Donna pursed her mouth. "Which is?"

"Let me ring Arnie Ash's place."

The name jolted like an electric shock through Kirstie's system. Tall red letters on a white sign above a wide gate. A feedlot behind a shabby main street.

"The abattoir?" Donna thought for a moment, casting a glance at the impossible gray mare with the unbreakable spirit. Midnight Lady stood head up, ears back.

"Yeah. They take horses and turn 'em into dogmeat," Leon said in a low, coarse voice. "It's not gonna be worth a whole lot, but you gotta admit, it's better than nothing."

5

"They're taking Midnight Lady down to the abattoir early tomorrow morning!" Kirstie spoke on the phone in a loud voice to Hadley. She stood in the booth inside the noisy End of Trail Diner, while Lisa leaned in through the doorway. Across the room, Matt was talking to Bonnie Goodman about what had happened.

"I hear you," Hadley replied. He offered no comment or opinion.

"Say something!" Kirstie begged.

"What do you want me to say?"

"Tell us what we can do to stop them!" It had been unbearable, listening to Donna Rose discuss the details with Leon Franks. The ranch manager was to call Arnie Ash and ask for a time when they could deliver the horse to the slaughterhouse; he was to drive the trailer himself to make sure that nothing went wrong.

"Get the best price you can," Donna had told him. That was her hard edge showing, a reaction to her disappointment that the money spent on Midnight Lady had been wasted.

"And next time let me choose my own horse," Leon had reminded her, with what both Kirstie and Lisa had thought was a nasty sneer.

On the drive back from Circle R to San Luis, Matt had told them they were both imagining things. "Leon's doing his job the best he knows how," he'd insisted. "Don't go reading too much into things."

"You never saw him sacking out," Kirstie had retorted. "The guy's got a mean streak. If I was Donna Rose, I'd watch out for him!"

"You want me to stop Donna from sending her horse to Arnie Ash?" Hadley said now.

"Ask him if your mom would like to buy Midnight Lady!" Lisa hissed, poking her head over Kirstie's shoulder. A couple of truck drivers came into the diner and began to order burgers and fries from Bonnie. Meanwhile, Matt was looking at his watch and obviously thinking of his date with Lachelle. He gulped down the last of his coffee and put the cup down on the counter.

"I heard that, too," Hadley cut in before Kirstie had time to repeat the question. "I can give you Sandy's answer without even asking her."

"Hadley, explain the situation to Mom. Say we'd only need to pay half of what Midnight Lady is worth." Kirstie knew that the price given by Arnie Ash would be rock bottom, and that Donna Rose might well be tempted by a higher offer. "And you know yourself what a good horse she is!"

Silence from the other end. In the diner there was the whirr of the till, the hiss and spit of cooking oil as Bonnie Goodman tipped a scoop of raw fries into the pan.

"I know what a good horse she *was!*" Hadley replied at last. "Past tense."

"What do you mean?" Kirstie put one hand over the receiver then turned her head toward Lisa. "He's gonna refuse to help!" she groaned.

"Midnight Lady was a great horse before Leon Franks and his pair of thugs got their hands on her." Hadley spelled it out. "But I don't hold out much hope for her after what they put her through this last week. I've seen what happens to a strong-spirited horse when she's been brutally treated. She gets this wild streak running through her: half-fear, half-anger. No way will she settle down and become a steady dude ranch horse. Her temperament's spoiled for good."

"Not Midnight Lady!" Kirstie protested for all she was worth. "She's special. She could learn to trust again."

"Hmm."

"Don't be like that. I know what I'm saying..." Desperately she broke off and turned to Lisa.

Lisa grabbed the phone. "Hadley, are you still there? What Kirstie's trying to tell you is she's already made friends with Midnight Lady. You know how great she is with horses. She only had a few minutes with her on Sunday afternoon, but she cut across all the cruel stuff, really got through to her. Beneath all that bucking and rearing, there's still a beautiful, gentle horse…"

Kirstie took back the phone. "At least ask Mom the question for me."

"Sure." The short answer conveyed his deep doubt that it would do any good. Then Hadley changed tack. "What does Matt say?"

Kirstie faltered. "You know Matt; always counting the dollars."

"Don't even think about it!" was exactly what he'd said. The words were etched in her brain.

"And you also want me to pass on the message that you plan to stay over at Lisa's place?" Hadley recalled. "Did I get that right?"

"Yeah," she sighed, her heart sinking. "Things work out best if I sleep here. Bonnie can drive me home tomorrow morning…"

Tomorrow morning, when it would be too late to save Midnight Lady, when the Circle R trailer would already have driven down Renegade's shabby main street, through the white gates, under the red sign to her short journey's end.

* * *

Three miles in complete darkness!" Lisa objected. "Kirstie, are you crazy?"

"We'll take flashlights."

"It would take hours to get there!"

"Not by bicycle. You ride yours. I'll borrow your mom's." Kirstie brushed aside the excuses. Doing something, anything, was better than doing nothing.

"What if someone sees us?" Lisa had a long list of protests up her sleeve. She was snuggled deep under her blankets in a warm, comfortable bed, and here was her crazy best friend talking about getting dressed again, going out into the cold and dark, sneaking off on bikes along Route 27, through Renegade, all the way to Circle R.

"Who?" Kirstie challenged. She was already unzipping her sleeping bag and climbing into her jeans and sweatshirt. "It's past midnight. Everyone is asleep."

"I wish *I* was!" Groaning and sighing, Lisa flung back her covers. "Why can't we be normal kids, Kirstie, listening to music, surfing the internet? When we have a sleepover, why can't we do just that—like, *sleep* over!"

In spite of everything, Kirstie grinned. Lisa looked funny with her dark red hair tousled and sticking up at the crown, her mouth pouted and sulky. "I could go alone," she suggested, guessing the response.

"Whoa, no way! You think I'd let a lunatic like you ride around the country by yourself!" Lisa pulled on her trousers, overbalanced, and hopped around the room.

"Shh! Your mom will hear!" Opening the bedroom door, Kirstie peered along the landing, then quickly backed off. "There's a reading light on in her room!" she whispered.

"No sweat. Mom always leaves that on all night." By this time, Lisa had succeeded in getting fully dressed. She rummaged in a drawer and brought out a flashlight, then tested it by shining it full in Kirstie's face.

"Thanks!" Dazzled, then blinking hard, Kirstie turned and set foot on the quiet landing. The boards creaked as, one step at a time, she made her way toward the stairs. Behind her, Lisa stubbed her toe and swallowed a sharp "ouch!"

"What if Mom wakes up and finds our beds empty?" Lisa hissed her final objection in the hallway at the bottom of the stairs. The neon light from the diner sign shone in through a narrow window, turning her face a sickly blue.

Kirstie considered it. Bonnie would panic and start making phone calls. Then, back at Half Moon Ranch, her own mom would freak out. They would probably bring in the police. But by then it would be too late to stop her and Lisa from carrying out their secret plan. "We risk it!" she decided, opening the front door and stepping out under the moonlit sky.

Sleek and silent, a weasel shot out from under a pile of logs and down a storm drain at the side of the road. A frog hung limply from his jaws; the long, black-tipped tail whisked as the weasel vanished down the narrow hole.

At the last moment, Lisa caught sight of him in the beam from the light mounted on the front of her bike. She turned her handlebars to miss the swift creature, wobbled, and fell sideways into Kirstie.

Both girls crashed to the ground, then picked themselves up unhurt. "How much farther?"

Kirstie whispered, scanning the flat, open land that lay ahead.

"About a mile." Lisa whispered her reply. She glanced back at the lights lining the main street of Renegade. It had seemed like a ghost town as they rode through. A dog had howled, a gate had swung open in the wind. No one had stirred.

"Why are we whispering?" Kirstie hissed as she got back on her bike. "There isn't a soul out here!"

"I know. Isn't it creepy?" Lisa drew a deep breath. "It's like being swallowed up by a giant black hole; like you ride by accident into a hostile universe and lose your way back into the daylight world of cars and shops. And all the people you ever knew wake up and wonder where you are.

"You're on this black planet with weasels and prairie dogs, and a million miles of grass, and you can see your folks, but they can't see you. Like there's this invisible wall between you and them. The sun and daylight is there, and everyone going about doing the normal stuff, crying because you vanished and they think you're dead. If only you could let them know you're OK. But you can't because you're locked inside this nightmare world..."

"…And eventually you give up like all the other victims who have ever vanished into the hole," Kirstie finished off. "You turn into a prairie dog, barking and whistling in the night, and are never seen again! Thanks for that cosy little bedtime story, Lisa!"

Pedaling slowly over the uneven track that would take them to the Circle R, the joke fell flat. The sky was too vast, the thing they were about to do too serious for them to stay lighthearted. And then the ranch itself came into sight; first the long, straight fences at the boundary of Donna Rose's property, then the house at the end of the dirt road.

"Are we absolutely sure that this is what we want to do?" Lisa stopped and put both feet on the ground. There was still time to turn around and go back.

"Certain," Kirstie told her. She got off her bike and propped it against the fence, ready for a quick getaway. This was going to be tough and scary, and there would probably be trouble at the end of it. Suddenly she felt guilty about having dragged her friend into it. "Honest, Lisa, you can stay here and keep watch. I can go ahead by myself!"

"Do I look as bad as you?" Lisa stared her in the face, taking a deep breath and deliberately ignoring the offer.

"White as a sheet," Kirstie confirmed. "With big, starry eyes. Like you're so frightened you can hardly swallow, and your heart's practically jumping through your rib cage!"

"That's me!"

"Me, too!"

Tilting back their heads, they both looked up at the sky. A million pinpricks of stars shone; the moon was a nibbled silver disc disappearing behind a wisp of gray cloud.

"Ready?" Kirstie asked, taking the flashlight out of her jeans pocket and striding toward the ranch.

The horses stood at attention in the meadow behind the barn. Their eyes gleamed, their coats glinted in the moonlight.

"One, two, three, four, five..." Kirstie counted out the hardworking sorrels used by Leon, TJ, and Jesse. She and Lisa were crouched beside the barn. The smell of creosote from the freshly painted wall filled their nostrils.

The nearest horse turned his head, ears cocked. His face looked black in the shadows, but there was that gleam of white as he rolled his eyes.

"There's Moonpie!" Lisa pointed out the gray gelding in the far corner of the field. He was wearing a head collar, staring over the north fence at the hills beyond Renegade, the start of the foothills that eventually became the Rockies.

"He looks weird in this light!" Kirstie whispered. Like a dream horse, a pale shadow.

"And Skeeter!"

Kirstie followed the direction of her friend's pointing finger to see the black-and-white paint break into a trot away from the main bunch. He joined Moonpie by the fence, as far from the crouching girls as he could get.

"Do you reckon they've seen us?" Lisa shifted position.

"Yep." No doubt about it. The horses had smelled and heard them from the beginning. They'd been alert, watchful, and ready to react at the first sign of danger.

"Should we move?"

"Nope." Not until they were sure that Midnight Lady

wasn't in the meadow. Once they'd checked it thoroughly, they would have to edge nearer to the ranch house and start searching inside the barn. Meanwhile, Moonpie and Skeeter seemed to be unsettling the five other horses, who broke out of their group and scattered to the far corners. Their hooves pounded over the turf, sounding to Kirstie and Lisa's oversensitive ears like a roll of thunder.

Kirstie flinched and crouched back behind the wall. She checked the upstairs window of the house; no lights went on, no one stirred.

"Leon must have put Midnight Lady in a stall for the night," Lisa whispered. "That way he can back the trailer right into the barn and get an early start in the morning."

A shudder ran through Kirstie. "Looks like it. You know something, we don't know where Leon and the other two sleep!" It bothered her that she couldn't identify exactly where they were.

"They must be in a bunkhouse somewhere. Maybe behind the ranch house?" Lisa shrugged. "We can't worry about that right now. Come on!" Still crouching, she turned and slid around the corner into the yard.

Kirstie followed. From this position they could be seen from the house, so they had to scurry fast toward the barn door. She held her breath until they were inside, then stood upright in the pitch dark to recover.

"Do you have the flashlight?" Lisa's voice was thin and quavery.

"Right here." Kirstie flicked the switch. A yellow beam picked out the row of wooden stalls, then the stack of hay bales at the far end of the barn. Her hand shook and the beam wobbled up to the rafters, across the roof.

"Hold it steady!" Lisa was venturing forward, listening for movements. If there was a horse in here, she would soon grow uneasy at the noises made by intruders. They would hear her stamp and snort.

"Last time we came, Midnight Lady was in the stall past the haystack!" Kirstie decided to venture farther in. "There's a door down there that must lead straight out into the meadow. Leon could have brought her in that way."

As she walked with the flashlight past the empty stalls, she grew more convinced she was right. The muggy barn felt like it contained a living creature, almost like there was breath in here, and warmth from a body. She swept the light up the stack of hay and down again, turned the corner, and shone it carefully into the final stall.

The beam fell first on the straw-covered floor. It lit hooves and slender legs, cast just enough light to pick out the shoulders and curved back, the arched neck, and long, straight face of Midnight Lady.

The horse stared out of the darkness without moving.

"Easy!" Kirstie whispered, keeping the beam out of her eyes, hoping that Midnight Lady would recognise her voice. "It's me, remember!"

The mare dipped her head and snorted, kept her gaze steadily on Kirstie as Lisa appeared at her friend's side.

"You didn't think we'd forgotten about you, did you?" Kirstie handed the light to Lisa then took a step nearer, noticing the tether tying the horse to a metal ring on the wall. She reached out to undo the knot. Her words seemed to have a calming effect, so she murmured as she moved in, saying, "Easy, we'll soon have you out of here. Hold steady while Lisa finds out how to unbolt this door... Hear that? That's the door swinging. Now you can feel that fresh air blowing off the plain... Yeah, nice and easy!"

Lisa's fingers had worked at the stiff bolts and slid them back. The hinges had creaked as the door opened. Midnight Lady smelt the cool grass and a thousand nighttime scents. She followed Kirstie's gentle lead toward the open air.

Outside, the seven horses bunched tensely in a far corner of the meadow. They watched and waited as Kirstie brought the gray mare out of her dark prison into the moonlight.

"OK, now comes the hard part!" Lisa looked along the fence from end to end. The meadow dipped to a stream at one end, but there was another strong fence on the far bank. Now she was certain there was only one gate, and it led into the yard by the house. That meant they had to lead Midnight Lady right under the nose of her sleeping owner.

"We'll do it!" Kirstie set her course toward the gate. "You know why?" she told the horse. "We've got this plan to help you escape. It's an emergency. No time to do anything sensible. The important thing is to get you out of here before morning!"

Once more, her voice kept Midnight Lady calm. The other horses had begun to stir and split off, swerving across the field, their manes and tails flying, their hooves kicking up turf. But not the gray mare; she came along sweetly, listening to Kirstie's words.

"We get you off the ranch, and tomorrow we think again," she promised. "Maybe the animal welfare people will get involved. Maybe I can persuade my mom to buy you after all..." They were waiting for Lisa to open the gate, their backs to the nervous herd, almost free.

Lisa slid another bolt.

A light went on in a window in the house.

Kirstie saw it. For a sickening moment, as her heart jumped and she held tight to Midnight Lady's lead rope, she prayed that the light would go back out.

But no. It stayed on. A figure came to the window to look out.

"Quick, Kirstie, get her out of here!" Lisa urged.

But the new urgency had spooked Midnight Lady. She pulled at the rope, veering away, back into the meadow. "Not that way!" Kirstie tried to stop her, felt the strength of the frightened horse, tugged in vain.

The rope stretched taut as Lisa urged Kirstie to be quick. Kirstie felt it burn her palms as it slipped. It was agony to hold on, and Midnight Lady was full of fear, ready to flee in exactly the wrong direction. One more wrench of her head and Kirstie had to let her go.

Now she could run. She was a flight animal. It was all she knew.

She reared and turned, joined the other horses in the meadow, screamed out a warning. Moonpie and Skeeter galloped to her, gathered her, and raced her off across the field. The ranch horses jostled and bunched after them. They thundered down the slope to the stream, splashed into it, turned and made a crazy dash toward a second fence and then a third.

"Get out of the way!" Lisa gasped at Kirstie as the horses swung toward the gate. She shoved her to one side, against the gatepost, leaving the opening clear.

Kirstie was down on the ground, staring up at the charging horses. They galloped rhythmically over the soft earth toward her.

Their hooves shook the earth, they reached the gate, and then they were through. Midnight Lady led them, pounding past Kirstie, who was struggling to her feet. Then came Moonpie and Skeeter, mad with the idea of freedom. They charged through the gate ahead of the ranch horses, who all followed the three broncs into the yard, raising dust, scattering in every direction.

More lights in a lean-to section of the ranch house. Kirstie saw them as she stood up. Her palms were burning, her cheek hurt where she'd fallen against the gatepost.

But the horses were still galloping, three across the flat land to the south, black shadows disappearing into the night.

Two circled the ranch house, then broke off in the direction of the town. In the dim confusion she spotted the black-and-white shape of Skeeter. He raised his head and found the jagged black horizon of the distant mountains.

Then she lost him in another whirl of activity.

Moonpie? Midnight Lady? Two pale horses disappearing into the night. Which was which? Where were they headed? She saw that both gray horses were tracking after Skeeter in his race for the mountains.

But everything was confused; her palms felt like they were on fire, voices yelled out of the darkness.

"Run, Kirstie!" Lisa cried, dragging her across the meadow, away from the house.

Kirstie followed, hardly aware of what she did.

And she didn't care. Midnight Lady was free; that was all that mattered.

6

"Lisa?" Bonnie Goodman called up the stairs to her daughter, thinking she was still fast asleep in her bedroom.

It was half past seven on Thursday morning, opening time for the End of Trail Diner.

Lisa was sitting fully dressed except for her jacket on the edge of her bed. Kirstie stood by the window with her sleeping bag draped around her shoulders. Her fair hair hung limply across her face, her gray eyes were dull. Neither had changed back into pajamas after the night's events. Both felt drained, almost numb with fear and guilt over what had happened.

"Lisa, come down! TJ and Jesse are here. They've brought some bad news from Circle R!"

Lisa groaned. "OK, we're on our way!" With an effort she stood up and went to pull back the drapes. "What now?" she asked.

Kirstie closed her eyes and shook her head.

"What do we do? Do we admit what we did?"

"If we do, we're in big trouble!" Until now, they'd hardly said a word to each other, as if speaking about it only made it worse. They'd run across the meadow under the cover of darkness, circled back to the dirt road, grabbed their bikes, and pedaled away unseen.

By that time, there had been no chance of re-capturing the eight escaped horses. As they'd rid-den off, Kirstie and Lisa had heard the sound of surprised, angry voices coming from the yard at Circle R—the ranch hands discovering the open gate and empty field. They hadn't stuck around then to own up, so why now?

"We're in big trouble anyway!" Lisa tried to be more realistic. "If we go down there and listen to

TJ giving us the bad news about their horses, we'll have to look like we're surprised and shocked. I don't know about you, but drama definitely isn't one of my best subjects!"

"So? We put our hands up and say it was us? What then? They'll call the cops." Kirstie pictured her whole world collapsing. The look in her mom's eyes when the local sheriff paid them a call. She didn't think she could face that.

Lisa took a sharp breath. "My mom will just die!"

"Yeah! Mine, too." On the other hand, they could decide to keep quiet and let everyone think it was an accident that the horses had gotten out. So much easier. So much less painful.

"...Lisa, Kirstie, are you coming down?" Bonnie called again.

"Why don't we just set out to find the horses?" Kirstie said hurriedly. "If we recapture them all except Midnight Lady, what harm is there in that?"

"Easy peasy!" Lisa's eyebrows shot up.

"It's not that difficult," Kirstie insisted. She could hear Bonnie's footsteps coming upstairs. "The ranch horses probably won't go far. They'll most likely hang around in the Renegade area, find some good grass. Come nightfall, they'll be making their way home."

"Which leaves the three broncs!" Lisa dashed to the door to intercept her mom. They still had no firm plan.

"Lisa!" There was a knock, a couple of seconds' pause, then the door opened. Bonnie peered into the room, a dish towel tucked into the waistband of her jeans, bringing with her from the diner the smell of bacon cooking and coffee percolating. "There's a problem at Donna Rose's place. The horses got out in the middle of the night. TJ and Jesse are asking for help for a search party. I said I was sure you and Kirstie would be willing..." She stopped short and stared at Kirstie. "Say, how did you get that bruise on your face?"

Kirstie's hand shot up to her cheek.

Then, puzzled and suspicious, Bonnie bent to pick up Lisa's blue padded jacket from the floor. She rubbed at a black mark, sniffed it, and frowned. "And where did this creosote paint stain come from?"

There was dead silence. Down in the parking lot, a car pulled up and new customers entered the diner.

Bonnie gazed in horror from one to the other. "Oh my gosh!" she whispered. Then her mouth snapped shut. She turned, went right down to the phone, and called Sandy Scott.

"And the worst of it is, you planned to lie!" Kirstie's mom was white with anger. She'd driven over to San Luis to collect her daughter and taken her home in silence.

Kirstie slumped into a seat at the kitchen table. Outside, the sun was shining, the sky was blue as usual. But everything else had changed utterly.

"And before you say it, Kirstie, keeping quiet, letting Donna think her horses had escaped by accident is the same as telling a lie!"

"I know." She was brokenhearted. The look she'd dreaded, the one that said, "You let me down big time!" was etched into her mom's face. "I'm sorry!"

"It's not enough!"

"I know."

"How could you do it? To me, to all of us!" Sandy didn't go into detail.

"I wasn't thinking straight. I just wanted to stop Midnight Lady ending up as dog meat!"

"And this is what comes of letting your heart rule your head, Kirstie!" Sandy flung her hat onto the table and turned her back. "What happens? It gets out of hand and leaves Donna with no working horses on her entire ranch. So how is she gonna work her cattle and keep her business going? She has wages to pay and three men who can't get on and do the work she's hiring them for!"

"Mom, I'm sorry!" Kirstie dragged herself to her feet without caring about the tears that were running down her cheeks. "Can't we lend Donna some of our horses until they track hers down?"

Sandy looked over her shoulder. "Say that again."

"We could trailer three horses over to Circle R for them to use. That way Donna gets to keep her ranch running. And I could say sorry face to face!"

Whatever it cost, that was what she needed to do right now, more than anything else in the world.

"This doesn't mean you're not still grounded for the rest of the vacation!" Sandy warned.

She'd said the plan was a fair one, that it went some way toward making amends for what Kirstie and Lisa had done. So they'd loaded Johnny Mohawk, Silver Flash, and Yukon into the trailer, left Hadley and Charlie in charge of the guests for the morning, and by ten thirty they were driving to Renegade.

"I know." Kirstie's reply was flat and monosyllabic. With every bend and dip in the road, she felt she would be sick.

"And Donna could still call the sheriff and press charges," her mom pointed out. "She could throw the book at you if she wanted!" And it would be no more than they deserved, she implied. There was no point turning to her, Sandy, for sympathy or help. Kirstie and Lisa would just have to take the consequences for their own crazy, half-baked plan.

Lisa, too, was grounded. Bonnie had yelled a lot and called her a "foolish girl!" She'd gotten on the phone with her own father, Lennie Goodman, to arrange for Lisa to stay with him for a few days. Sending Lisa up to her grandfather's at Lone Elm Trailer Park was meant to keep her out of trouble until the Circle R horses had been tracked down and recaptured.

"Meanwhile, we're minus three of our best horses at Half Moon Ranch and Hadley's having to reorganize mounts for some of the guests, and all because..." Sandy broke off and sat tight-lipped, her hands gripping the steering wheel.

Across the lights from them, pulling out of the abattoir gates in an empty pickup, was Leon Franks. He didn't notice them, but the sight of his thin, bony face was enough to remind Kirstie what all this had been about. And why had he been to Arnie Ash's place? Had Midnight Lady been found and taken there to be destroyed as planned? Her blood ran cold at the thought and she shrank back into her seat.

Sandy eased across the road and soon turned off for Circle R. Kirstie recognized the sudden expanse of flat prairie land, the tiny ranch at the end of the straight track, growing bigger as they approached. She scanned the landscape for signs of the runaway horses, saw only black-and-white cattle raising their heads and looking blankly after the trailer as it trundled by.

They were at the ranch house before she had time to gather her thoughts and get over the idea that the battle to save poor Midnight Lady might already be lost. The door was closed, the porch empty except for the chilies and the antlers. The whole place had a sad and slightly run-down air, she noticed for the first time.

Sandy hadn't said a word since breaking off her sentence at the Renegade traffic lights. Now she left the cab and slammed the door, taking a deep breath before she made her way onto the porch to knock at the door.

Kirstie attempted to swallow. Her mouth and throat hurt with the effort of trying not to cry.

No answer. Sandy tried again.

This time the door opened. Donna had obviously looked through a window, recognized her visitors, and been unable to understand why they and the trailer were here. She held the door half-closed, peering suspiciously around the edge. Kirstie watched her mom's explanation, the shrugs, the apologetic gestures, the earnest conversation. Gradually Donna opened the door wider and she came out onto the porch.

"No, really!" the ranch owner was saying, shaking her head, glancing at Kirstie still sitting in the passenger seat. "There's no need. It's a great gesture on your part, but I couldn't accept... It really isn't necessary!"

Slowly Kirstie slid out of the passenger seat. The ten feet of dusty ground she had to cross to the porch felt like miles. Her feet were lead weights on the end of weak, trembling stalks.

"One of the horses has already come back of her own free will," Donna was telling Sandy.

Which one? Not Midnight Lady, please!

"Wildflower, one of the ranch horses," Donna went on.

Kirstie breathed again. Leon Franks hadn't taken Midnight Lady to the abattoir after all.

"She just came back nice and gentle in her own good time," Donna said. "Leon expects some of the others to do the same before the day's out."

"Use our horses anyway!" Sandy insisted. "Even if the others do come back, they'll need resting. Johnny Mohawk, Yukon, and Silver Flash are all fresh and ready to do some work." Behind her back, Sandy gestured for Kirstie to hurry and join her. "Anyhow, Kirstie has something she wants to say," she told Donna.

Kirstie dragged her gaze from the step where she'd planted her feet, across the worn boards of the old porch, until it made contact with Donna's fancy brown and cream boots, her blue jeans, her silver buckle, all the way up to her face. Then she blinked in surprise. The face wore no makeup, the streaked blonde hair was uncombed. It was Donna Rose without the mask; tired, middle-aged lady with a lost look in her red-rimmed eyes.

"I'm real sorry!" Kirstie whispered.

Donna studied her face. "Yes." She nodded, then looked even more lost than before, murmuring, "I just wish I understood!"

"I'll help find the horses!" Kirstie promised, desperate to make things right. "I know which way they headed. I can tell TJ and Jesse where they should look!'

"That would be good." Donna nodded vaguely, gazing out across the plain as if expecting to see the lost horses trotting obediently toward home. Then she turned to Sandy and gave her a weak smile. "Don't feel too bad. Your girl evidently had a reason for doing what she did."

This got worse and worse. Kirstie hadn't expected the sad resignation in Donna's manner; anger would have been easier to deal with. "I didn't mean to let all the horses escape!" she tried to explain. "Only Midnight Lady!"

"Ah yes, the gray mare." With a shake of her head and another sad smile, the old lady turned back to Sandy. "I appreciate your wanting to help me with the loan of these horses," she told her. "But it may not make any difference in the long run."

"How come?" A determined Sandy went to the trailer to begin unloading Silver Flash.

Donna followed and helped to lower the ramp. Inside the trailer, the horses whinnied and moved restlessly about the confined space. "What I mean is, this latest—incident—" Donna glanced at Kirstie, "is only the last in a long line of problems. Ever since Don died I've had to struggle to keep things going. He went suddenly, see, and no way was I prepared for running the ranch single-handed. It had always been the two of us; Don and Donna Rose of Circle R. Him working the cows and running that side of things, me keeping house. Old-fashioned maybe, but that's the way we liked it."

"It's tough doing things single-handed," Sandy agreed. She went into the trailer and led Silver Flash down the ramp. "You have to give it everything you've got."

"It's kinda late in life for me to learn how to do that." Donna stood to one side. "My answer was to hire a manager, which I couldn't really afford, but it seemed the only way to stay on here."

Sandy handed over the big sorrel with the white blaze to Kirstie and went back inside. "But then, good hired help is hard to find."

"I've had three managers in as many years," Donna admitted. "This time, I had to go out of the state as far as Wyoming to find Leon. And the problems don't end there. Money for feed; that's my biggest headache. And the ranch is pretty run-down; there's more money needed to put the fences in order, for instance. Not to mention work on the house and barn." She turned to Kirstie, who had tethered Silver Flash and come back to collect Yukon from her mom. "So in a way, your crazy little plan of last night helped me come to a decision."

Kirstie frowned. "It did?"

"Yeah. It made me realize it may all be too much for me to handle. Like, one last straw that broke the camel's back."

Sandy came out of the trailer with Johnny Mohawk, a pretty black half-Arabian and the final horse that she wanted to lend to Donna. She stopped on the ramp, sensing an important announcement.

The lady ranch owner looked away into the distance once more. "Too many problems, not enough money...and then, suddenly, out of the blue just before you arrived, an offer to buy the place! Add it all up and what do you get?"

"Someone wants to buy Circle R from you?" Kirstie repeated. Just when lending Donna the three horses was helping to salve her guilty conscience, she was hearing the news that she planned to give up. Now Kirstie felt really, really terrible again.

"What are you saying?" Before Donna could answer Kirstie's worried question, Sandy came down the ramp, shaking her head in disbelief.

"I've had an offer!" Donna repeated, her lips quivering, her eyes filling with tears. "Not a great offer, it's true. But it's a cash deal; money on the nail."

"Have you accepted?" Sandy asked gently.

"Not yet. I told them I'll think about it."

"Told who?" Kirstie demanded, looking Donna Rose full in the face for the first time that visit. "Who made the offer? Who put in the bid to buy Circle R?"

7

"Arnie Ash called me. I just got off the phone five minutes before you pulled into my yard." Donna seemed to be trying hard to get her muddled thoughts in order. "Well, I knew he was loaded; the slaughterhouse does good business. But I never knew he had that kind of dough. A cash offer!" she repeated.

Kirstie frowned suspiciously. "Why does he want to buy the ranch?"

"Why not?" Sandy seemed to think it was a reasonable idea. "It would be a good thing for him if he went into cattle ranching, raised his own cows and so on. There could be a lot of extra profit in it for him."

"Especially if he modernizes," Donna conceded. "He'd keep a manager in place who would bring everything up to date."

"Manager?" Kirstie echoed. Her brain ticked over faster than before.

"Sure. He said he hoped Leon would stay on after I sold up. I haven't had the chance to talk to Leon yet..."

"That figures!" *Tick-tick-tick.* Leon Franks had been driving out of the abattoir as they went past. He'd been looking pretty smug. So that was what he'd been up to, running to Arnie Ash to tell him about Donna's problems, encouraging the slaughterhouse owner to move in on the widow with a cheap offer. Yeah, of course!

"Kirstie, don't interrupt!" Sandy said sharply.

"Sorry." She frowned down at her feet. Now was not the time to explain her theory. But she thought it through. "Hit the old lady while she's down!" Leon must have told Arnie Ash. "She can't handle this latest crisis of her horses running off. Right now she'd listen to any offer, even if it was peanuts!" Arnie Ash would get the best deal of his life. He'd be grateful to Leon for the inside information. Leon would probably be rewarded with a good raise in pay.

Bad news. Terrible news, in fact. Made all the more real by the fact that Leon's pickup was approaching the ranch house right now. He sped over the bumpy track and swung into the yard with a squeal of brakes, slamming the door and giving Sandy and Kirstie a long, hard look.

"Why the trailer?" he demanded.

"We loaned Donna some horses until she gets hers back." Sandy's voice sounded defensive.

"Who asked you to do that?" Glancing angrily at Johnny Mohawk, Silver Flash, and Yukon, Leon lifted his leather chaps out of the back of the truck and began to tie them on.

"No one asked us. We thought it was the least we could do." Realizing that they'd outstayed their welcome, Sandy headed for the trailer. "Keep them as long as you need to," she told Donna.

"You gotta realize these aren't real ranch horses," Leon cut across Sandy and Kirstie's path to warn his boss. "They're used to dude ranch work, carrying amateur riders out on the trail, not professional cowboys cutting out and roping cattle."

Kirstie stopped in her tracks. "Hey. Johnny Mohawk is as good as any cutter or roper on Circle R!"

Leon sneered at her. "In your dreams!" He went across to the dainty black horse, who backed away at his sudden approach. He laughed outright at Johnny's slim build. "Are you saying this weakling can hold his ground against a fifteen-hundred-pound steer, or work up enough speed to rope a calf?"

"Sure!" Kirstie refused to back down. "Arabians are pretty fast, and they're known for having a lot more stamina than a quarter horse." Her heart was thumping with a mixture of anger and anxiety. It didn't take much imagination to guess how Leon Franks would treat the Half Moon Ranch horses while they were here. She saw the cowboy's spurs glint in the sun and watched Johnny Mohawk pull back to the limit of his halter rope.

"C'mon, Kirstie," her mom said, looking worried

herself. She said good-bye to Donna, who had stood nervously on the porch since Leon's arrival, as if working up enough courage to break the news of Arnie Ash's recent offer to him.

For another few moments, Kirstie hesitated. "How long have you got before you have to give Arnie an answer?" she murmured quietly to the elderly ranch owner. She noticed Leon Franks hovering rudely on the edge of their private conversation.

Donna sighed and shook her head. "Not long. He said the offer was only good for a short while, otherwise he would put in a bid on another ranch he's been looking at lately."

"But how long exactly?" Kirstie knew that an awful lot hung on Donna's answer.

There was the dim, distant look in her eyes, a catch in her throat as she replied. "Twenty-four hours," she whispered. "Arnie wants a decision from me by this time tomorrow morning!"

"TJ and Jesse just found two more of their horses!" Hadley greeted Sandy and Kirstie with good news.

It was midday when they finally got back home,

having driven the trailer along the back roads around Renegade and San Luis, searching for the missing animals. They'd looked along the banks of Horseshoe Creek, in meadows hidden behind copses of willow and aspen. Once, they'd spotted movement: a reddish brown creature stumbling through marshy ground. They'd left the trailer and tracked the animal on foot, coming across it as it drank from the creek.

"Bovine!" Sandy had said quietly, using the jokey cowboy term.

The cow had raised her white head, water still dripping from her blunt pink nose. The brand on her rump showed a capital R inside a circle.

"She's Donna's cow, but she must have wandered off ranch property," Sandy had decided. "C'mon, girl; yip, yip!"

They'd spent the best part of an hour driving her out of the culvert and back onto Circle R land.

Arriving home to Hadley's news, Kirstie was the first out of the trailer. She followed him into the barn. "Any idea which two horses?"

The wrangler tossed alfalfa hay into wooden feed troughs, then watched as three foals scrambled across the pen behind the barn. Their sticklike legs and heavy heads made their progress ungainly. But soon they were tucking into a good feed. "Two more ranch horses," he reported. "A sorrel named Foxy and an appaloosa named Pilgrim."

"Where did they find them?" For a few seconds, the cute foals had taken Kirstie's mind off the problem. The biggest, a black-and-white paint, was head-butting the palomino and the bay to get at the best of the hay. But then the other two ganged up to cut the paint out. In the end, they all seemed to agree there was enough for everyone and settled down to munch contentedly from the manger.

"To the south of the ranch," Hadley told her. "Leon reckoned they'd head across the plain rather than cut back toward the mountains. Seems he was right."

Kirstie gave a small nod, then turned away. She had a flashback to the night before, seeing in her mind the moonlit scene, when the horses had split off in all directions: some toward the flat lands to the south, it was true, but some toward Eagle's Peak in the north. Skeeter, for a start. Probably Moonpie and Midnight Lady had followed close on his heels. But she said nothing to Hadley about that.

"Kirstie!" Her mom called her from the house porch.

She broke into a run, along the dark corridor of wooden stalls, past the round feed bins, through the heavy pine door into the corral.

"Lisa's on the phone!" Sandy waited, arms folded. "You two are grounded, remember! Don't go making plans!"

Nodding, Kirstie scooted by to take the call in the kitchen. She arrived breathless and curious.

"Hey." Lisa didn't sound her usual bubbly self.

"Hey!" She perched on the edge of the table, staring out at the mountains.

"I'm up at Lone Elm. I just heard from Grandpa; they found three of Donna's horses so far."

"I know." News traveled fast. "Donna's thinking of selling Circle R."

"What! I never knew that."

Not that fast, then. There was a long, awkward silence for her friend to start feeling guilty in. "Did you call me just to tell me about the three horses?"

"No, really..." Lisa seemed to be making a decision to say what was on her mind. "Kirstie, I just

110

drove up to the trailer park with Grandpa. He's pretty mad at me."

"The whole world is mad at us," Kirstie confirmed. "So?"

"So, he wasn't saying much. I spent the whole time looking out of the window, making like I didn't care."

"You and me both." Lisa was having the same kind of hard time as she was, Kirstie realized. "So, is there a point to this story?"

"Well, I couldn't swear to it," Lisa sighed. "Maybe I'm a bit crazy right now. But we were driving up to Lone Elm and Grandpa stops to talk to the Forest Guard. I'm seeing loose horses everywhere, like, not really seeing them, just imagining them."

"It's because we didn't get any sleep last night."

"Well, whatever. They mostly turn out to be shadows or mule deer. Finally, I'm looking up at a rock, seeing what I think are three horses on the skyline. Grandpa is saying good-bye to the Forest Guard. I'm saying, 'Hold on a second!' but he's deliberately ignoring me. So I'm trying to work out if this time it's more mule deer, or if it really is three horses. One's definitely a black-and-white paint..."

"Skeeter!" Kirstie gasped.

"One's too far away to know if it's a flea-bitten gray, but I'm nearly sure..."

"Moonpie!" Kirstie lowered her voice to a murmur.

"And the third one, another gray, is looking down from the rock, watching me watching her. She's wearing a head collar, and her ears are up, and she's staring, ready to run..."

Kirstie closed her eyes and almost stopped breathing. "Midnight Lady!"

"I guess so. But I can't do anything because Grandpa's refusing to listen to me. He's driving on and the sound of the engine spooks them. We take a bend to the left, through some trees, and when I look up again the horses have gone. I'm staring up at an empty rock. Zilch. Nothing!"

"Can you remember which rock?" Kirstie begged. She glanced over her shoulder to see her mom standing in the doorway.

"Angel Rock," Lisa whispered back.

Then something must have happened at her end of the line. Suddenly there was a click, and the phone went dead.

That afternoon, Sandy booked Kirstie's horse, Lucky, into one of the trail rides and planned a list of chores for Kirstie which would keep her busy until nightfall. Beginning with logs. She had to help Charlie to stack the wood in the back of a trailer and deliver it to each of the guest cabins. Then there were horse blankets to hose down, scrub and clean, before slinging them over the corral fence to dry. After that, there was tack to clean, bales of hay to shift, yards to rake, and the tack room to sweep.

"I'll stack the hay," Charlie suggested. It was two thirty and he saw that Kirstie looked exhausted. "You catch up on some sleep."

Sandy was out leading a ride up Coyote Trail. She wouldn't be back until five o'clock. "Are you sure?" Kirstie checked her watch.

"Sure I'm sure." He took a heavy bale from her and set off across the barn. Then he hesitated and glanced back. "Just make sure you stay out of trouble, OK!"

Charlie must have sensed that Kirstie's brain was racing and that sleep was the last thing on her mind. So she made a quick exit before he could withdraw his offer.

Angel Rock! It was beyond Lone Elm Trailer Park, on the far side of Miners' Ridge. How could she get over there without a horse? Or should she risk saddling Charlie's horse, Rodeo Rocky? No way. The tack room was next to the barn where Charlie was working. Could she grab a rope instead, lead Rocky out of the meadow, and ride him bareback? That way she was much less likely to get caught. Stopping by the house to think, Kirstie realized this was the best way.

Soon she had slung a rope across her shoulders and was slipping over the bridge toward Red Fox Meadow. Rodeo Rocky was the only horse in there, since every other horse on the ranch was in use or out on loan. He looked up and whinnied as she approached.

"Ssh!" Kirstie climbed the fence and jumped into the field. The bay horse's coat shone with its peculiar metallic glint in the full sunlight. His dark mane and tail hung silky smooth. Quickly she reached out to clip the lead rope onto the head collar, then led him quietly out of the meadow.

The next move was more difficult. Rodeo Rocky was a brave and intelligent horse, one they'd rescued from San Luis Rodeo where they'd found him being badly treated. Once wild, he'd now learned to trust Kirstie and was a wonderful ranch horse, Charlie's pride and joy. But he was young and strong, and had no experience of being ridden bareback. It was possible that as soon as Kirstie tried it, the strangeness would make him kick and buck. She could soon be thrown to the ground and trampled by the panicking horse.

Leading him out by the creek, away from the house and barn, Kirstie waited until they reached the cover of some willow bushes before she stopped and made her first attempt to talk gently to the horse, persuading him by her voice and gesture, that whatever she was about to do wasn't intended to frighten or hurt.

"I wouldn't ask you to do this if I didn't have to!" she whispered, looping the lead rope around his neck.

Rodeo Rocky dipped his head and snorted. He shook himself from head to foot.

"This is gonna seem kinda strange," she went on. This time, she ran her hands over his neck and shoulders as she talked. She felt him watching her carefully. "I know you like a saddle and bridle, so that you're familiar with what's going on. But just for today, we're gonna have to do without."

I'm listening, he said by the turn of his head, the flick of his ears. *Go ahead.*

Kirstie found a nearby rock to raise herself from the ground and bring herself level with the horse's head. Then she rested both arms across his left shoulder. Leaning against him, she felt him brace himself to take her weight. "Now, I'm gonna grab a fistful of mane and haul myself up," she warned. "Once I get my leg over your back, you have to stand nice and easy. Otherwise I get thrown off, see!"

She was breathing the words into his ear, slowly easing herself into position. Rocky stood fast, obviously wondering what she was up to, but prepared to trust her.

Smooth and slow, Kirstie slid her leg over his broad back. She pushed herself upright. "Easy!" she murmured, as Rocky felt her full weight. She kept hold of his mane, kicked gently, and clicked her tongue.

He took a step forward, then another, swaying as he climbed the slope away from the creek. When he found that Kirstie slipped from side to side without her saddle, he tried to even out his stride. And without the usual bit and reins to guide him, he saw that he must pay more attention to her legs and voice.

Using her heels, she asked him to take Meltwater Trail, slowly at first, finding her balance, gaining confidence. Rocky listened hard. He got used to the novel sensation of being ridden bareback.

"You're doing fine!" she murmured, as they passed by a stream that fed the creek. "What do you say we try a trot?"

Rocky agreed. He broke his steady walking gait, picked up his feet, and set off uphill at a smooth trot. Kirstie rose and fell, one hand on his shoulder, one hand holding the looped lead rope.

"And how about a lope?" she breathed.

Rocky felt her sit down firmly and make the kissing sound that told him to go faster. He stretched his strong legs into a steady lope.

With the wind in her hair, swerving by pine trunks and through copses of silver green aspens,

Kirstie covered the ground. The sun dappled the earth, the breeze shimmered through the trees. She was riding bareback, getting as close to nature as it was possible to be.

8

Less than an hour after her spur of the moment decision to check out Lisa's sighting of the three missing horses, Kirstie and Rodeo Rocky reached Angel Rock.

The outcrop of pinky gray granite had appeared on the skyline as they skirted wide of the entrance to Lennie Goodman's trailer park, and Kirstie had kept it in view ever since. Of all the rocks around, this one most lived up to its name, she thought. Sure, Hummingbird Rock was a great label for the outcrop that attracted the tiny, darting birds that sucked nectar from the wildflowers growing all around. And Bear Hunt Overlook was good for the flat ledge of rock where the hunters of old had stood with their guns, searching for black bears and their valuable pelts. But Angel Rock, shaped like the angel you would put on top of a Christmas tree, complete with wings, was the most perfect name of all.

Strong sunlight picked out the shape of the angel's face in profile, shadows played a fluttery trick and made the wings move as Kirstie approached up the final slope.

"Whoa!" she whispered to Rocky.

It was baking hot, silent except for the clip of the horse's hooves over the gravelly ground.

When he came to a standstill in the shadow of the rock, Kirstie slid from Rocky's back and tethered him to a tree. She listened carefully. More silence, seemingly miles of it as she gained the ridge and gazed into the next valley.

"Skeeter, where are you?" she whispered. "Moonpie? Midnight Lady?"

"Hey!" A figure stepped out suddenly from behind Angel Rock.

"Oh, Lisa, you scared me!" She recognized the wild red hair and freckled face of her best friend, noticed the coils of rope hanging from her shoulder. "What are you doing here?"

"The same as you, I guess."

"B-but… How come you didn't tell me what you were planning?" Kirstie had caught her breath and recovered from the shock.

"I didn't get the chance. Grandpa heard me talking about Angel Rock and ordered me off the phone. I had to make up an excuse to get away, so he didn't suspect anything."

Kirstie nodded. "Likewise." Excuses and pretenses, and more trouble if they were found out. "They'll think we planned to meet up here."

With a shrug, Lisa turned her attention to the tree-covered slopes of the valley. "I just felt I had to help Donna get her horses back, that's all."

"You know what they say about great minds." She and Lisa had thought alike. "I'm hoping that if we get her horses back to her before tomorrow morning, she'll change her mind about selling the ranch."

Still scanning the hillside, Lisa nodded. "Would that include Midnight Lady?" she asked quietly.

Kirstie frowned. To take the unbroken gray horse away from these peaceful hills, back to the torment of Leon Franks's sacking out would break her heart.

"I take it that means no," Lisa said after a long pause, setting off downhill through the tall, dark trees.

They searched for half an hour without success. If the horses really had been to Angel Rock, they'd left no sign.

"OK, so I imagined it!" Lisa sighed, pushing her hair back from her hot face, then fanning herself with her wide-brimmed hat.

The girls had scoured an area within a half-mile radius of Angel Rock, and come full circle back to the place where Kirstie had tethered Rodeo Rocky. It was time to give in and go home.

The bay horse seemed pleased to see them, snorting and pawing the ground as they returned. He raised his head and pricked his ears, as if expecting to be untied.

"OK, OK, don't get too excited," Kirstie told him.

His ears were flicking in every direction, then he curled his lips and let out a long, high whinny. She was on the point of loosening the slipknot when a second horse replied.

"You hear that?" Lisa gasped. She froze and listened.

Down in the valley toward Lone Elm, the mystery horse whinnied again. This time it seemed closer.

"What do we do?" Lisa demanded. She'd scrambled onto a rock and was staring in the direction of the agitated cry.

"Wait here!" Kirstie decided. She felt that pretty soon Rocky's call would attract the other horse to Angel Rock. His herd instinct, together with natural curiosity, would draw him

Sure enough, the dialogue continued. Rocky would whinny to give the stranger his position, the invisible horse would reply.

"He's getting closer!" Lisa murmured, searching hard for movement on the tree-lined slope. At last she was able to point to a shape gliding through some aspens, reluctant to show himself, but tempted on by Rocky's dominant call.

Kirstie saw him. Almost as pale as the slender white trunks of the aspens. A gray horse.

"Moonpie!" Lisa recognized the brown-specked, flea-bitten coat.

The horse moved clear of the trees. Yes, it was Moonpie and not Midnight Lady. Kirstie heaved a sigh of relief. "And Skeeter!" she whispered, as a second horse drifted between the tree trunks. The black-and-white paint was easier to spot and identify. Both horses wore head collars and approached without fear, eager to make contact with the tethered bay.

"Wait!" Kirstie murmured again. There was no need to do anything dramatic. Thanks to Rodeo Rocky, Donna's newly broken broncs were simply walking back into their arms. She turned to Lisa to take one of the ropes which she'd slid from her shoulder.

In her mind's eye she already had Skeeter and Moonpie safely attached to a lead rope. She and Lisa were walking the horses down to the trailer park. They would call Circle R and wait for Donna to send up a trailer to collect them...

The sound of an engine cut into the hot, heavy

peace. Rocky tried to rear, but his tether pulled him down. Moonpie and Skeeter turned up the slope in sudden panic.

A pickup truck was racing up a jeep track between the trees. It skidded to a halt and two men jumped out. They raced through the undergrowth toward the confused horses, cutting off the escape route they had chosen by crowding them into the shadow of Angel Rock.

"Hey!" Kirstie yelled a protest as she recognized Leon Franks and TJ. "There's no need for that!"

They ignored her, moving in with ropes of their own. They swung lassos over their heads, sending them snaking through the air toward the horses' heads. Both landed on target and were jerked tight around their necks.

"We said there was no need!" Lisa was angry. She stormed up to Leon, while Kirstie did her best to calm Rodeo Rocky. "We could've brought them back nice and gentle!"

"We believe you!" Leon sneered, heaving on the rope to force Moonpie down the hill. "Like, you're the reason we've got this problem in the first place, remember!"

Lisa's mouth snapped shut, she blushed bright red, changing tack, and running after TJ and Skeeter. "How did you find out where they were?" she demanded.

TJ struggled to control the black-and-white horse, whose eyes were staring, his whole body resisting capture. "We got a call from Lennie Goodman," he muttered, dodging a sideways kick. "We drove over as fast as we could."

"And what are you gonna do with them?" Lisa had to stand to one side, out of the way of Leon and Moonpie.

"Look, kid, just beat it!" The ranch manager's shaky hold on his temper gave way as he tried to steer the gray horse toward the truck. "Go on, get out of here!"

He lashed out with his free arm, knocking Lisa backward against a tree. Kirstie heard the thud and ran to help her up.

"Are you OK?" She pulled her to her feet.

Lisa held on to her shoulder. Her face had turned pale, but she nodded.

"Nightmare!" Kirstie hissed. She turned to see the ramp at the back of the truck clatter to the ground and Leon Franks using his full weight to shove Moonpie inside. "No way is that safe!"

Grimacing with pain, still holding onto her arm, Lisa turned away. "The sooner this is over, the better!" she agreed.

It was TJ's turn to force Skeeter into the truck. He tied the horse to a metal bar behind the driver's cab, alongside Moonpie. The two horses stamped and pulled, sweating with fear and barging against each other in the confined space.

"If they get them back to Circle R in one piece, it'll be a miracle!" Kirstie predicted, disgust in her voice. She hated every inch of Leon Franks's bony, sharp, cruel frame.

He raised the ramp and slammed it shut, then ran to the cab, where TJ was already sitting in the passenger seat. There was a roar from the engine and a puff of black smoke from the exhaust. The sudden jerk forward sent Moonpie and Skeeter into a fresh frenzy. The last glimpse Kirstie and Lisa caught of them through the cloud of smoke was of two horses arching back and kicking, squealing for all they were worth.

In the silence after they'd gone, Kirstie felt her spirits sink lower than ever before. There didn't seem to be a move she could make without Leon Franks suddenly appearing. Then all her good intentions toward Donna Rose would vanish and she was left only with the sour taste of disgust.

And now the man had hurt Lisa with his bad-tempered shove.

"Let's get you back to the trailer park," she offered, untying Rodeo Rocky and waiting for Lisa to join her on the jeep track. "Can you get up on his back?"

"No, I'm fine, thanks." Lisa's tense, pale face suggested otherwise.

"You're not fine. I'll walk you to the gate at least." That's where they would split up and Kirstie would begin to make her way back to Half Moon Ranch and who knew what new problems there. By then it would be around about five, the time when her mom was due back from her trail ride.

Nodding grimly, Lisa agreed to the plan. They set off slowly together, Kirstie leading Rocky, each dreading what would greet them when they got home.

"Look on the bright side." After half an hour's mostly silent walking, as the entrance to Lone Elm came into view, Lisa managed a faint smile.

"What bright side?" As far as Kirstie could see, there was none. "We're both about to be grounded for the rest of our entire lives, and here's you telling me to think positive!"

Clutching her arm, trying to smile, Lisa looked back the way they'd come at the hillside deep in shadow. "The sun's still shining on Angel Rock," she murmured.

"Yeah?" Not enough to make her feel better.

"And Midnight Lady is still up there somewhere!"

"Yeah!" Kirstie nodded. The light at the end of a very dark tunnel. Midnight Lady. Still free.

Kirstie had to keep that in mind as she and Rocky retraced their steps to Half Moon Ranch. A horse like Midnight Lady could survive quite well in the mountains, even though she was alone now. She would forage in the small meadows she would find by wandering down culverts. There would be plenty of clean water in the rushing streams. Come October, when the snow began to fall, it might be a different matter. But winter was a long way off.

Deep in thought, she rode Rocky along Meltwater Trail. She was managing for the first time to picture a long-term future for the brave gray horse, reassuring herself that there was no animal living in the Meltwater Range that would pose any real threat to Midnight Lady so long as the horse managed to stay healthy and uninjured. Coyotes and wildcats would keep their distance. A bear and her cubs that had been sighted in the area earlier that year had since moved on.

True, Midnight Lady would be lonely. A herd animal needed others around it, so maybe she would move on before winter came and blocked the mountain passes. Ancient instinct might tell her of wild horses on the Wyoming plains and lead her far away. Kirstie might never see her again.

Sadly she rode Rocky down from the hills and onto the jeep road that crossed Meltwater Trail. They were only about half a mile from home when she noticed clear tire marks in the dust, a sign that this was probably the route chosen by Leon Franks with the two recaptured horses. The tracks snapped her back into the present. Where was the pickup truck now? Had it already reached the main route into San Luis? Were Moonpie and Skeeter still safe?

"Call it premonition!" Kirstie said later.

It was dusk. The vet, Glen Woodford, had raced out to the scene as soon as Charlie had called him. Kirstie was standing next to her mom, gazing at the smashed pickup, its front end buried into a rock at the side of the road.

"I just knew they were never gonna make it!"

She and Rocky had come down to Five Mile Creek, on the last stretch before they reached the ranch. Something had made her turn and glance up a steep track to the right, the one that Leon Franks would have to have taken to get to Route 5. And there they were. The wheels of the half-upturned truck were still spinning, Leon and TJ were climbing out of the cab, going around the back to check on the injured horses.

Without stopping to find out the details, her heart practically bursting through her ribs, she'd turned and raced for the ranch house. Charlie had met her in the yard and managed to calm her down. She'd pleaded with him to call the vet.

"It's Moonpie and Skeeter! They've been in a crash. I think they're hurt real bad!"

It had seemed like forever, but had only really been half an hour before Glen had gotten here. Sandy Scott had arrived back from her trail ride to find chaos: Charlie giving orders to Leon and TJ that no way should they try to get the horses out of the back of the truck before the vet came, Hadley riding up and demanding what the hell was going on, Kirstie still shaking and faint with shock.

But now things were under control. Kirstie watched Glen climb into the truck with a syringe full of sedatives for the horses. It was difficult to see in the fading light, but he seemed to be calming Leon and telling him that the injuries didn't look too bad after all, that it was mostly shock, together with minor cuts and bruises. The drug was beginning to take effect. Soon it would be safe to get Moonpie and Skeeter out of the truck onto firm ground.

Sandy Scott heard and took a deep breath. She strode over to Leon and reminded him that he should call Donna with the news about what had happened. "Tell her the horses are gonna be OK,"

she insisted. "And Kirstie, go with him to show him where the phone is."

"Yes, ma'am." That was it, an order not to be disobeyed.

Scowling, feeling the skin at the back of her neck prickle, Kirstie led Leon Franks toward the ranch.

9

"It was a busted tire," Leon reported, glaring at Kirstie as he spoke into the phone. It was as if he was daring her to contradict. "That old truck is a deathtrap. We're lucky it didn't turn into something worse."

A busted tire—not! Inwardly Kirstie fumed. More like dangerous driving by Leon, showing off in front of TJ. His carelessness made her blood boil.

"It'll take a heap of money to fix it," he went on. "Then there's gonna be Glen Woodford's bill on top of the garage repair bill."

Don't listen to him! Kirstie paced up and down the porch, hearing Leon pile on the agony for Donna's benefit.

"And hey, we don't know yet if the horses are gonna have to be destroyed. It looked to me like Moonpie got a busted leg. He could end up at Arnie's place, and maybe Skeeter, too."

Over my dead body! For every lie that Franks told his boss, Kirstie had an instant, furious but silent comeback.

"...No, don't you do that, Donna." Leon's tone changed. He grew more cagey and shielded the receiver with his hand. "No way. You stay right where you are!"

Kirstie stopped to one side of the doorway, listening hard.

"...No, listen. What's the point of you driving all the way out here? I can handle things."

Yes, come! Kirstie thought. *See for yourself what's happening and find out the lies Leon tries to push.*

"...OK, OK! I hear you. Sure, they're your horses.

You have every right to see them." Leon gritted his teeth. "Only, you have a whole heap of things on your mind right now, and I reckon I can handle things here." He tailed off and put the phone back on the hook. "Suit yourself!" he muttered.

Staying out of sight, Kirstie heard Leon's footsteps set off across the kitchen, then halt. There was a pause, before he hurried back to the phone, picked it up and dialed.

"Arnie? Hi, it's Leon."

Pressing herself against the wall, Kirstie leaned closer toward the open door. This was obviously something he didn't want anyone to hear.

"Yeah. You want the bad news first? Well, Madam Rose still hasn't made up her mind to sign the paper. *Will I? Won't I?*" He mimicked a high, fussy voice, then went on with a mocking tone. "You know how she is. But the good news is: today she has more bi-ig problems!"

Kirstie frowned as he described Donna's latest troubles, making light this time of the damage to both truck and horses.

"It couldn't have happened at a better time if we'd actually planned it!" Leon laughed. "It's gonna push her closer to the edge. She won't get any sleep tonight, so tomorrow morning, when you show up waving a nice fat check in her face, you can bet your life she'll sign that old contract!"

Yeah, it was as Kirstie had suspected. Leon was in league with the abattoir owner. And there was more to come.

"You want some more good news?" he gloated. "Remember the gray mare I was gonna bring in first thing this morning? Yeah, the one that those two kids wanted to rescue. You were gonna pay Donna peanuts for her, selling her the story that the horse would end up on the butcher's slab? Yeah, that one."

In the pause that followed, Kirstie's brain raced. It sounded as if Leon and Arnie had been up to more crooked stuff.

"What happened to the real buyer on the cattle ranch out in New Mexico that you had lined up?"

She narrowed her eyes and tried to work it out.

"Is he still interested? Yeah? You get a good price and we split the profit two ways? . . . OK, well the deal's on again!"

How come? It was impossible. Midnight Lady was still missing.

Leon laughed at what must have been a puzzled response from Arnie Ash. "Listen. I was up at Angel Rock. We got word that's where we'd find the other two broncs. And sure enough, we found 'em and loaded 'em into the truck. The fool kids got in the way again, but we soon got rid of them. Anyway, it must be my lucky day! We're shooting off down the track, with old Moonpie and Skeeter kicking up a fuss in the back. We come around this bend, through some trees and along Miners' Ridge. Hey, and guess who we nearly ran into?"

"Midnight Lady!" Kirstie whispered out loud.

"You got it!" Leon drawled into the phone. "The gray mare. She rears right up and turns down into the canyon, full gallop. First chance I get, I'm heading back there to throw a rope around her pretty neck and bring her in!"

As the sun went down and a pale half moon rose in the clear sky, Kirstie stayed in the background.

She'd slipped away from the house at the end of Leon's gloating conversation with Arnie Ash, so that the ranch manager had no idea that he'd been overheard. And she'd kept quiet as Charlie and Sandy had brought Moonpie and Skeeter into the corral, supervised by Glen Woodford, with TJ hanging back at the rear. She'd watched the vet rub an antiseptic cream onto the horses' cut knees and faces, shuddering slightly to see blood still oozing from the raw gashes.

Then, when Donna Rose had driven up to the ranch and stepped out of her car, Kirstie still said nothing. She was watching, listening, waiting for her chance.

"Gee, I'm sorry!" Sandy greeted the older woman with genuine sympathy. "So much has gone wrong these last twenty-four hours, you must feel as if the whole world is against you!"

"Pretty much." Donna looked worn out. She walked over to Glen Woodford, who was packing his bag, ready to head on to his next call.

"You can breathe again," he told her gently. "As far as I can tell, there are no bones broken and only superficial traumas."

Donna nodded and sighed heavily, going across to Skeeter and patting his neck.

"I've given them a couple of shots: tetanus and

an antibiotic. But really, all these guys need from now on is a big dose of TLC!"

"So how much do I owe you?"

Glen waved the question to one side. "Later."

"No. I like to pay my debts right away," Donna insisted.

"OK, I'll get my secretary to write you a bill. Meanwhile, you check your veterinary insurance. You'll probably find you're covered." Glen zippered his dark green jacket and smiled kindly. He shook hands with Donna, then Sandy, before climbing into his black jeep. He leaned out of his window. "Hey, and make sure it's Leon who drives that beaten-up old truck back to Renegade!" he warned. "Charlie and TJ managed to get it back onto the track a while back, but if anyone's gonna break his neck after the way he must have driven that thing, let it be Leon!"

Donna managed a smile. "You've been great, Glen. Thanks." As the vet drove off, she went to pass on his message to her manager, who nodded dourly and began to search in his pockets for the ignition key. Meanwhile, Donna went around the dark yard thanking Charlie and then Sandy.

"We'll keep Moonpie and Skeeter for a couple of days until their cuts heal up," Sandy suggested. She insisted on Donna, Leon, and TJ coming into the house for coffee. When Donna protested, she overrode her. "No, really. You keep Johnny Mohawk, Silver Flash, and Yukon at Circle R. That'll work fine, I promise!"

"But I'll send Leon over in the morning to drive the truck back, if that's OK," Donna told her. "The headlights are all smashed, so no way can he drive it in the dark. He and TJ will have to come home with me tonight."

It was all fixed in a friendly way while Sandy asked Kirstie to serve the steaming coffee.

And still Kirstie waited and listened. *Good!* she thought, when she heard the plan. That gave her a few hours' grace. For though her body went through the motions of pouring coffee into cups, her mind and heart were out on the moonlit mountain with Midnight Lady.

"I don't mind admitting, I'm whacked!" Donna sighed, staring at her own reflection in the dark window, trying to tidy up her lank hair by pushing it behind her ears.

"It's been quite a day," Sandy murmured. Then, "Has it altered how you think about Arnie Ash's offer?"

"Some," Donna confessed. "I tell you, Sandy, if that pen had been in my hand and the contract on the table in front of me when Leon called and told me about the accident, I'd have signed it then and there!"

Kirstie stood with coffee pot poised over Leon's mug. She noticed a nerve flick under his eye. Yet he tapped the table casually with his forefinger, pretending to play the drums, as if he was no part of the ongoing conversation.

"But?" Kirstie's mom prompted. "How do you feel now?"

"Better," Donna sighed. "So now, half of me is saying, yes, sign the deal with Arnie. It makes sense to give up the ranch rather than struggle on. And yet..."

"I know. There are memories wrapped up in the old place." Sandy interpreted the pause.

"Don loved Circle R," Donna said simply. "It was his life."

She stood up from the table and walked to the

door, lost in thought. Letting her go, Sandy turned to Leon and TJ to arrange the details of picking up the truck next morning.

"If we still have a boss!" TJ said, sourly pointing out that by then everything could have changed.

Leon said nothing, but kept on drumming his fingers on the table.

Kirstie watched Donna drift out onto the porch, then down into the yard. The moon shone bright as she crossed slowly to the corral and Kirstie followed. She came up beside the old lady as she looked in on Moonpie and Skeeter, then up to the horizon and the dark summit of Eagle's Peak.

"Memories!" Donna whispered, as she grew aware of Kirstie at her side. Evidently she held no grudge for the trouble she and Lisa had caused. "At my age, that's pretty much all you have!"

For a few moments, Kirstie hardly dared to break the silent moonlit spell. Then the dream she'd been nursing since she'd overheard Leon's talk with Arnie Ash, broke through. "If..." she began softly, then paused.

Donna smiled down at her. "If what?"

"If I could bring Midnight Lady back and make everything right again. . .if I could turn things back to the way they were before all this happened, would it make you decide to stay on at Circle R?"

10

"That daughter of yours is a sweet kid," Donna told Sandy. She'd cried a little, told Kirstie that it was a kind offer, but not one that she could fulfil. The horse was missing, and anyway she was too hard to handle. No way could anyone bring her back without using force. She'd sighed, squeezed Kirstie's hand, and gone back into the house.

"Sweet?" Sandy echoed, raising her eyebrows but sounding grateful as well as surprised. "Since when?"

Kirstie gave an embarrassed grin as she cleared away the coffee cups. Her mom was right, "sweet" was definitely what she was *not!*

But the two women were getting along great. Donna more or less admitted that the original problem over Midnight Lady was partly her fault; she hadn't supervised Leon's breaking in methods closely enough, had left the running of the ranch too much in his hands. And, to Kirstie's surprise, she didn't seem to care that Leon was overhearing this. The ranch manager scowled but didn't dare to protest, since for the first time Donna demonstrated who was boss.

It was Sandy's idea that Donna should stay over at Half Moon Ranch. "You're tired," she reminded her. "Let Leon and TJ drive your car back to Circle R, help Jesse look after things at that end. They have to come back in the morning to collect the truck. By that time, you'll have had a good night's sleep and things may look a little brighter."

There were more scowls from Leon as a grateful Donna accepted the offer. "Arnie Ash wants an answer early tomorrow," he reminded her.

"I'll call from here." Donna's mind was made

up about the overnight stay. She waited for Leon to follow orders.

The arrangement gave Kirstie the space she needed to put things right once and for all. She wouldn't try to explain or persuade; instead she would *act!*

First she had to wait for Leon and TJ to drive off and for Donna and her mom to finish chatting and go to bed. She had to fight off her own exhaustion, splashing cold water over her face and leaning out of the window to gulp in fresh air after she'd said her good nights and gone up to her room, where the bed in the corner had looked soft and tempting.

Hunting through her closet, she chose a thick fleece and a baseball cap to protect her from the chilly night. But she shouldn't leave her room too soon. She must wait until her mom and Donna were asleep. The minutes seemed long as she checked the clock: half after ten, ten forty-five, eleven.

Then at last, when the house was silent, she crept downstairs. She went outside onto the porch, pulled on her boots, then tiptoed out in the yard, glancing back at the bedroom windows.

This time she would risk taking a saddle and

bridle out of the tack room, keeping a close eye on the bunkhouse where Hadley and Charlie were already asleep. She hoped! Heaving the saddle from its hook, she breathed heavily and wondered why she'd put on so many clothes. She was too hot. It must be because her nerves were playing up, and because the saddle was heavy as she carried it out to Red Fox Meadow.

By the time she got to the fence, her knees had begun to buckle. She dropped the saddle in the grass and softly called Lucky's name.

So far the plan was going like clockwork. Lucky came eagerly to her call, his mane and tail almost white in the moonlight, his dark eyes gleaming. Soon he was saddled and ready to ride. "Meltwater Trail!" Kirstie murmured as she slipped her foot into the stirrup and swung onto his back. "We're going to Miners' Ridge and Dead Man's Canyon. C'mon, Lucky, let's go!"

Kirstie felt certain that she and Lucky would find Midnight Lady at the end of their moonlit ride. She knew horses and how they were likely to behave. The gray mare would follow her herd instinct and still be hanging out in the area where she'd last seen her companions, Skeeter and Moonpie. That meant starting the search at Dead Man's Canyon and making their way up to Angel Rock. There, under the trees, or in the deep black shadows of the rocks, Midnight Lady would be waiting.

But what would she do, how would she react when she saw Kirstie and Lucky? Would she recognize Kirstie as the girl whom she had trusted, who had set her free from Leon Franks's ropes and tarps? Or would her experiences at Circle R have soured her nature and turned her against all humans? As she rode Lucky into the narrow entrance to Dead Man's Canyon, Kirstie understood there was no way she could possibly predict the answer to this most important question of all.

After a few wary steps into the deep, dark ravine, she reined Lucky to a halt and listened. She heard but couldn't see the waterfall at the far end of the canyon, the call of owls, and the distant, barking cry of a coyote. Kirstie glanced up at the sky, waiting for thin, ghostly clouds to clear, and for the moon to shine fully into the canyon. Lucky shifted and scraped his feet on the rocky ground. He turned his head, waiting for the next command.

"OK, she's not here!" Kirstie decided. "Let's try higher up!"

They were retracing their steps, passing through Fat Man's Squeeze, when Lucky hesitated and looked up to his right onto Miners' Ridge.

The moon was out in a clear sky, the silvery light picking out every blade of grass, every tiny blue columbine that grew in the crevices between the rocks. Kirstie tilted her head and peered up the slope.

The runaway horse gazed down, her legs and body in shadow, but her neck and head white in the moonlight. Her eyes were deep, dark pools.

The midsummer sun rose before six on Friday morning, tipping the mountains with golden pink light while the rest of the valley lay cold and gray.

It was decision day for Donna Rose.

"You're up early," Donna said to Kirstie, when she came down to make coffee. The lines on her face seemed deep and careworn, there were shadows under her eyes.

"You, too." Kirstie hugged her secret, tried not to race ahead.

"Yes, I didn't sleep well." Donna forgot about coffee and drifted toward the kitchen door. "It's a beautiful day!"

"I guess you were trying to decide about the ranch," Kirstie said gently.

Donna glanced around. "I'd say I changed my mind a hundred times at least. Fifty reasons to stay. Fifty reasons to go."

"And how about I give you the fifty-first reason to stay?" Now; before Sandy, Hadley and Charlie were awake, before Donna had the chance to call Arnie Ash and accept his offer!

"You're sweet…" A sad smile crept over Donna's features; she was shaking her head.

Now! though Kirstie's nerves were stretched tight, though she still couldn't be sure how this would work out! Everything depended on Midnight Lady.

"Come outside and take a look!" she whispered.

Donna had reluctantly agreed to play along, as if humoring Kirstie was a way of shelving her big decision one more time. "You kids have so much energy!"

she'd sighed, following her into the corral, where the resident pair of blue jays pecked in the dust.

The birds had flapped and squawked at their approach.

Then Kirstie had left Donna in the corral and slipped through the heavy pine door into the barn. Now she breathed in the nighttime, moist, musty smells of hay and sleeping animals, passing the stalls occupied by the three young foals and turning into the one where Midnight Lady had spent most of the night.

The gray mare was already awake and suspicious of the footsteps approaching her stall. True, she'd met Kirstie and Lucky on the mountain the night before and decided they were friend, not foe. She'd responded to Kirstie's kind words and come along calmly enough. Sweet alfalfa had tempted her into the barn, and the prospect of a clean, soft bed. But would it be the same in the cold light of day?

"Hey!" Kirstie said softly. She stopped in the doorway, avoiding eye contact, waiting for Midnight Lady to decide.

The horse looked intently at her. *Have you come to get me? Are you gonna take me some place with ropes and tarpaulins? Do you want to break me and destroy me like others of your kind?*

"Yeah, I know you're not sure," Kirstie whispered. Still she stayed where she was. "And I don't blame you."

Still gazing at her, Midnight Lady lowered her head. She licked her lips and ground her teeth. *Maybe, maybe…*one small step…*maybe!* She walked slowly to join Kirstie.

Yes! Kirstie felt a thrill of triumph. This was the third, magical time that the horse had accepted her. Once at Circle R, then last night on the mountain, and now! But she did nothing to disturb her, backing smoothly out of the stall, watching her follow. When Midnight Lady joined her again, she reached out and stroked her softly between the eyes. "Will you come and show Donna what a great horse you really are?" she whispered.

Midnight Lady dipped her head and followed again, past the stalls with the foals, along the dark passageway toward the square of daylight and the open door. No lead rope, nothing. Just the trust between girl and horse.

"Oh my!" Donna Rose saw them step through the

doorway into the corral and a shaft of early morning sunlight. Kirstie's fair hair fell in wisps across her tanned face, her white T-shirt hung loose over her worn jeans. The gray horse towered over her but followed her every move.

And now! Did she dare? Kirstie walked toward the saddle she'd positioned carefully on the fence. Would Midnight Lady take it? She had the memory of Leon, Jesse, and TJ's one, cruel attempt to saddle her, like grit, like sharp glass in her mind. If Kirstie attempted it now, would she buck and kick and go crazy as before?

Carefully, still without rope or lead, she lifted the saddle and slid it onto Midnight Lady's back. The horse's ears flicked warily; she blew through her nostrils. Bunched muscles in her jaw and neck showed that adrenalin was shooting through her, but, as Kirstie stooped to fix the cinch, she stood quite still.

"Goodness, who would've believed it!" Donna breathed from her position by the fence.

"I would, for one. If you'd have asked me, I'd have told you this girl could do it!" a voice said quietly.

Kirstie glanced up to see Hadley leaning on the fence, one foot on the bottom rung, his hands clasped comfortably along the top. The wrangler must have heard the jays kicking up a fuss and come out of his bunkhouse to find out why. She allowed herself a small, embarrassed grin.

"She has a kind of way with horses," he told Donna.

"It's magic!" Donna was shaking her head in disbelief as next Kirstie took a bridle from the fence post and gently slipped it over Midnight Lady's ears. The horse accepted the cold snaffle with a small lift of her head.

"No. It's what we call gentle breaking," Hadley murmured, watching keenly, ready to criticize if Kirstie made a wrong move. "The mare's doing fine, see; she's an OK horse."

"Easy!" Kirstie murmured, forgetting her audience, looping the reins over Midnight Lady's head. "We're gonna have fun, OK?" It was time to adjust the cinch and try putting a foot into the stirrup.

The horse felt the strap tighten and Kirstie's weight in the stirrup. She sidestepped nervously.

"Easy!" Kirstie waited, then swung her other leg over. That movement, the slow motion swing of her leg, the settling of her weight in the saddle, seemed to go on and on. The sun glinted on the silver snaffle rings, a sudden breeze lifted the silky hair of Midnight Lady's white mane.

The moment after, when the horse could so easily have bunched her muscles, gathered her strength, and exploded across the corral in a series of bucks and kicks, she turned her head to glance at Kirstie. This was all new and strange, but the look showed she didn't mind in the least. *OK, let's have fun,* it said.

* * *

"No regrets?" Sandy asked Donna.

The kitchen was full of the smell of bacon, eggs, pancakes, coffee. There were people coming and going in an endless stream.

Leon Franks had driven over from Circle R, and Donna had made her vital phone call to Arnie Ash.

"No regrets!" she replied, smiling at Kirstie, who tucked into a blueberry pancake drowned in maple syrup.

"Sure?" Sandy double-checked as she put plates of cooked breakfast in front of Hadley and Charlie. She'd been busy bringing Matt up to date with events after he'd arrived back from Denver, telling him about his sister's success with Midnight Lady.

"My only regret is that I didn't stop to listen to Hadley any sooner!" Donna announced.

Hadley ducked his head, grunted, and got on with the important business of food.

"I was such a fool to trust Leon!" Donna went on. The truth about his link with Arnie Ash had come out when she'd finally confronted him by the Scotts' corral. With his back against the wall, he'd finally been forced to own up to the fact that the slaughterhouse boss's offer had been for many thousands of dollars lower than Circle R was worth. And when Donna had told Leon he was no longer to be her manager, he'd accepted the decision without a word.

"What did Arnie Ash say when you turned him down?" Kirstie asked between mouthfuls. Gosh, she was hungry! So tired, so happy! Donna was gonna keep her ranch and Midnight Lady. She was gonna let Hadley find her a new manager: "The *second*-best in Colorado, mind!"... "So, who's the first?" Kirstie had cut in... "Why, Hadley of course! But I can't steal him from you, so he'll have to find me the second-best!" Donna hadn't heard her question above the bustle of activity. "What did Arnie say?" she repeated.

"He said I was crazy," Donna reported, a broad smile on her face. "I told him, I'd rather be crazy, thanks! Looking to the future, not the past, living in the place I love!"

"Me, too!" Kirstie agreed. She would finish these pancakes, then call Lisa at Lone Elm. "Hey, Mom, am I still grounded?" she asked as she dashed to the phone.

"Huh? Oh, I guess not!" Sandy was on her

way out of the house to organize the morning's trail rides.

"...Hey, Lisa!" Kirstie said, enjoying her friend's shrieks of surprise down the line. Through the window she could see Hadley, Matt, and Charlie tacking up the Half Moon Ranch horses in the corral. Beyond them, Donna Rose's dapple gray mare was happily grazing in Red Fox Meadow. "How's your shoulder? You wanna try and ride Midnight Lady before Donna takes her back to Circle R?... Yeah, really! You just ask your grandpa and get that butt of yours over here!"